Abby's Second Act

by

Melissa Klein

This is a work of fiction. Names, characters, places, and incidents are either the product of the author's imagination or are used fictitiously, and any resemblance to actual persons living or dead, business establishments, events, or locales, is entirely coincidental.

Abby's Second Act

Contact Information: info@thewildrosepress.com

Cover Art by *Diana Carlile*

The Wild Rose Press, Inc.
PO Box 708
Adams Basin, NY 14410-0708
Visit us at www.thewildrosepress.com

Publishing History
First Edition, 2021
Trade Paperback ISBN 978-1-5092-3662-6
Digital ISBN 978-1-5092-3663-3
Previously Published – 2013 The Wild Rose Press

Published in the United States of America

Dedication

To my biggest supporter, cheerleader, and very own Prince Charming. Eric, thank you for your support while I pursued my dreams and for believing in me before I believed in myself. You are my happily ever after.

Chapter One

"I hadn't planned on my hair looking like Medusa's snakes."

Holding a hand full of curls in place with one hand, Abby Roberts frantically shoved pins in with the other. Another tropical breeze wafted in from the open hotel balcony stirring the hem of her pink robe against her ankles and sending tendrils of blond hair fluttering against her neck. It beat the cold December rain she'd left in Atlanta, but it wasn't helping to tame her hair. She called over her shoulder. "A little help here, please."

Chris Mueller eased out of the chair where he sprawled, bringing along the pitcher of mimosas in one hand. After topping off her glass, he grabbed the loose pins from the dresser. "Being an architect doesn't make me capable of ensuring the structural integrity of your updo."

"You knew what you were getting into when you offered to keep me company."

She blasted the French twist with hair spray before shifting her attention back to her best friend. With sandy blond hair and green eyes, Chris had the all-American good looks going for him, and his graphic T-shirt and jeans only added to his easy charm. If he hadn't been brilliant at refurbishing old homes, he'd have made a killing as a model. "You could hang out with Jackson and his best man if you want."

He winked. "And miss hanging out with my best girl? Not a chance! This is your day almost as much as his."

She smiled at his reflection in the mirror. "I did pretty good raising Jackson on my own, didn't I?"

"What happens next?" He downshifted from the humor they'd been using to settle her prewedding nerves.

They'd had this conversation often enough for her to recognize the preamble. "We're due downstairs for pictures in thirty minutes."

He shot her one of his penetrating gazes. "You know that's not what I mean."

For a while she'd used the wedding as an excuse. Other than the changes that came along with today's events, she wasn't ready for anything more—and that included dating. "Don't you need to get dressed? Besides, you could take your own…" The staccato rap on the door interrupted her.

She looked through the peephole and groaned. There was no way to avoid this so, taking a breath, she opened the door to her sister. After an air-kiss in the direction of Abby's cheek, Sarah strode into the room, her mile-high heels stabbing into the carpet.

Abby visualized them sinking into the beach sand during the wedding ceremony.

What was she thinking?

Sarah pointed to the pitcher of mimosas with one perfectly manicured nail. "Starting the celebration a little early, aren't we?"

"I have a lot to celebrate." Abby walked to the dresser and raised her glass to her lips. "I could fix you a glass if you like."

"Hardly." Sarah crinkled her petite nose before turning to rest her gaze on Chris.

Abby eased over to link an arm through his. "You remember my friend, Chris Mueller."

Sarah smirked. "I remember. Didn't you wear sherbet-colored shirt to Jackson's law school graduation?"

Chris pressed his lips together. "The very same." He motioned to Sarah's dove gray dress. "You certainly look chic today."

Sarah offered him a plastic smile that didn't reach her eyes, then turned to Abby. "Why aren't you dressed?"

Abby skittered across the hotel room and snagged the garment bag on her way to the bathroom. "Just getting ready to." Jeez, she hoped she hadn't sounded like that when she'd used the same words on Chris earlier.

Hurrying so she didn't leave Chris with Polly Perfect any longer than necessary, she opened the garment bag and pulled her dress off the hanger. She'd gone over budget by more than a hundred dollars and would never have the occasion to wear it again but the color was her favorite shade of blue. She slipped it over her hips then reached behind for the zipper. It moved an inch. Dresses with zippers in the back weren't made for single women.

"Need help?" Chris called through the door.

"I've got it." No sense giving her sister something else to fume over. She sucked in her breath and gave the zipper a determined tug.

With her dress finally in place and her shoes and

jewelry on, she gave her reflection another once over.

There were a few laugh lines at the corner of her eyes, but the girls were as high as they'd ever been. Although considering she could see forty in her rearview mirror, perhaps she ought to think of her boobs as the women. "This is as good as it gets," she whispered then stepped back into the room.

Chris's face split into a wide grin. Too bad she didn't get the same reaction out of her sister. Judging by the purse of Sarah's lips, once again Abby had fallen short of the mark. "What?" She looked down to see if she had the dress tucked inside her panties.

"As the mother of the groom. You should have worn beige or at least chosen a more subtle color." Sarah's eyes stopped at a point just above the top of Abby's dress. "And shown a little less cleavage."

True, a good bit of skin showed between her neck and the neckline of the dress but she'd be darn if she'd let her bossy, older sister get under her skin. "Katie was with me when I bought it so it's bride approved."

Her answer didn't satisfy Sarah, but anything short of matronly modest would never be good enough in her sister's eyes regardless what the bride thought. Abby grabbed her purse and wrap then headed to the door. "The sunset won't wait on us. We're due downstairs in fifteen minutes."

Sarah stepped into the hallway and as Abby moved to join her, Chris tugged her back. His eyes were as penetrating as ever but the crooked corners of his mouth softened his expression. "Don't let her dampen your day. You look stunning." He brushed a strand of her hair back in place. "You're gonna have to beat the men off with a stick."

Abby's lips quivered as she suppressed the laugh bubbling up. "You crack me up. I haven't had a date in two years. My son's wedding is hardly the place to find one."

****

The notes of classical music ebbed, followed quickly by a burst of polite applause. Grant Davis' anxiety spiked as if someone was about to push him from an airplane and he knew there was a hole in his chute. It had been his honor to walk his baby sister, Katie, down the aisle. He only wished he'd been able to talk her out of his participation in what came next.

After giving his mother a peck on the cheek, he eased around the table to meet the bride and groom on the dance floor. Jackson offered him a handshake then stepped away. Katie looked up at him, her smile growing wider as he held his hand out to her. When the first notes began, Grant assumed the stance he'd practiced repeatedly but still couldn't master.

How can I catch, throw, or hit any type of ball, but when it comes to moving my feet in time to music, I'm a complete dud?

He managed the first steps and dared to hope he could make it through the next few minutes without making a fool of himself. Then he blew it.

Katie winced as his foot came down on hers. "I see six weeks of dance lessons didn't turn you into Fred Astaire."

The fifteen years separating them hadn't stopped the exchange of verbal jabs. "Thanks to that wedding planner you sicced on me at least I can dress like him."

"You look very nice." She brushed the shoulder of his suit. The transformation hadn't stopped with the clothes. The stubble he often let grow for days was gone and his hair was cropped close to his head. He looked more like a wealthy business owner than a jet jockey. Both titles were accurate but the only suit he voluntarily put on was his flight suit.

"Anything for you." He meant the statement down to the bottom of the oxfords he was dying to take off. Two people had the power to crack through his tough hide: Katie and his three-year-old daughter, Grace. One look at her in the delivery room and he swore off motorcycle racing for good. "Besides this might be my only chance to be father of the bride."

Katie slowed their dance from the sweeping waltz they'd been attempting. A serious expression replaced the dreamy look she'd been sporting all day. "Grace will get married someday, and if you don't kill yourself on your motorcycle, you'll get to do this all over again."

Grant appreciated her optimism. "I hope so." However, he doubted he'd ever get that privilege. A diagnosis of autism had changed his hopes for Grace. He purposefully pulled his thoughts from what might never be. "What am I supposed to be doing now?"

"Twirl me around like we practiced. Then at the end of this song, you dance with Mother."

"After that I'm off the hook?" He didn't bother to cover the hopefulness in his voice.

"We went over this at the rehearsal." Katie's reprimand held little weight when a grin threatened to give her away. "You and Abby have to dance." Katie had choreographed every minute of her wedding, from the bridesmaids' brunch that morning to the midnight fireworks on the beach to usher in the New Year.

"Then I'm off the hook."

"Until time to pay the bill."

Giving Katie the wedding of her dreams meant as much to him as it did to her. "Sounds like a bargain to me."

"Did I tell you thank you?" A serious tone replaced the banter that had bounced between them. A few tears shimmered in her eyes.

Preferring jokes or even bossiness to her seriousness, he gave her a spin. "Yes, about ten times yesterday and twice this morning."

She shook her head then gave him a playful swat, but warmth filled her voice. "After this, Jackson and I intend to fend for ourselves."

Just because she was getting married didn't mean he was done looking after her. "But you haven't bought a house yet."

"You have your own problems to worry about." The warmth and smile were still evident on her face, but there was finality in her voice.

The Davis family had a stubborn streak when they set their sights on something, and he had to admire his sister for wanting some independence. "Just promise you'll let me know if you ever need something."

The corner of her eyes crinkled and her lips quirked up at the edges. "What I need is for you to get your size thirteens off my toes."

Ten minutes after handing Katie off to a groomsman, Grant's ordeal was nearly over. "Try not to make a spectacle of yourself when you dance with Miss Roberts." Katherine Davis looked up at her son, her lips thinned in a strained smile. She'd spent their dance fuming over being upstaged by the groom and his mother. Going by the Cajun two-step the pair had done, they obviously knew their way around the dance floor.

"That's my goal every day, Mother." Grant followed the statement with a kiss on the cheek hoping to cover some of the sarcasm that had leaked out.

As he crossed the empty dance floor, he slid his hands into his pants pockets where he'd placed a cotton handkerchief. His old man hadn't been good for much, but he'd given him this trick to dry off his sweaty palms.

Two down, only one more to go.

He couldn't remember anything specific about Jackson's mother. He hadn't been paying attention last night at the rehearsal, and he'd had to slip out to take calls from work during the dinner she hosted. He headed over to one table in the ballroom where he didn't recognize any of the faces.

Of the three women, one was barely out of her teens. That left two who were huddled in a deep conversation and hadn't noticed him come over. He aimed his query at the woman facing him since she looked about the right age to have a son in his mid-twenties. "Mrs. Roberts, may I have this dance?"

Both women stopped talking. The one who'd had her back to him turned to face him. Her whiskey-colored eyes lined with a fringe of dark lashes caught his attention first. As she stood to take the hand he offered, all he could think about was how the color of her hair reminded him of ale, rich and full. "It's Ms. Roberts and since we're not in school, please call me Abby."

She certainly didn't look like any of his teachers. He might have enjoyed school more if they had. He hadn't wrapped his arms around anything this lovely in the two years since Heather had divorced him.

The band struck up the first notes of *The Way You Look Tonight* and he moved them towards the center of the dance floor trying desperately to remember if there were three or four steps to the foxtrot. His feet might not have remembered their job but his arms didn't need coaching. His hand slipped around her waist as if it was the most natural thing in the world.

Suddenly there was more at stake than family honor. He *wanted* to dance with this woman. If only he could remember what his feet were supposed to do.

Abby must have sensed his hesitation. "Wait until the next measure then start on your left foot."

He met her gaze. Her smile made everything, from the monkey-suit to the dance school torture, worth it. She didn't only smile with her lips, which were full and a sultry shade of crimson but also with her eyes that snapped with pleasure. He followed her instruction and everything jelled.

"You're getting it." She gave him another reassuring smile. "Slow, slow, quick, quick. You're a fast study."

"Not really. I think you ought to lead for a while."

"You're doing fine. Stop trying so hard and listen to the music." Her throaty chuckle made him want to say something else amusing, but he obeyed her instructions. He'd heard Sinatra sing the old standard a hundred times and never cared for sentimental lyrics. But, *man,* the rhythm wasn't perfect, especially considering the way her hips swayed gently with the beat.

They moved around the dance floor without

speaking. Her wide smile had softened and she had a distant look in her eyes. He imagined he carried the same look when he rode his sport bike.

God, he wanted to spend more time with this woman.

Is it socially acceptable for me to ask out Katie's mother-in-law? Aren't we related now?

He looked at her serene smile, thought about how good the creamy skin of her bare back felt against his hands, and decided all she could do was say no.

"I was wondering…"

She turned her attention to him and the spark in her eyes made him hopeful. But a tap on the shoulder cut off his question.

A portly man with jowls like a basset hound stood next to them. "May I cut in?" Words Grant never thought he'd dread hearing.

Abby's grip on Grant tightened. "Did my sister send you over here?"

The guy nodded. "Yeah." Then he grinned. "All the same I'd love to have a turn around the dance floor with the prettiest girl to leave Marietta."

Grant knew bull when he heard it. He opened his mouth to tell the guy to get lost, but Abby smiled and let the man ease her from Grant's arms. Before the pair moved away, she glanced over her shoulder, winked, and mouthed, "Thank you."

Chapter Two

"Must you be the belle of the ball at every event?" Sarah's words came out as a hiss.

Abby could hardly call the waltz she and her brother-in-law, Tripp, had done as an attention grabber. "Excuse me?"

From the corner of her eye she watched her niece, Jessica, slip away from the table. Abby would've made a break for it too if she could. A wedding was hardly the place to air old family issues.

Tripp patted his wife's arm. "Sugar, calm down."

If peacemakers really did get a heavenly blessing, this man had a lot to look forward to when he died. Abby appreciated his attempt to pacify her sister, but Sarah didn't look as if she planned on being mollified.

She jerked away from her husband's touch. "I will not. I could die of mortification."

Abby's temper warred with her sense of decorum. She leaned across the table and lowered her voice. "Why, because I was dancing? It is a traditional part of most weddings."

"It's not tradition for a grown woman to dance like that at her son's wedding. Katie's brother is at least ten years younger than you."

"Well, I can hardly help that.'

Chris grabbed her knee at the same time he wrapped his arm around her shoulder. She sank back into her chair and let out a long sigh. There was no winning with her sister.

Tripp looked in Abby's direction, flashing her one of his jowly grins. "I thought Abby looked very pretty out there. She dances nearly as well as when she won that scholarship to Julliard."

Good goodness why did he have to remind Sarah of that?

She smiled at him all the same. "Thank you. The dances were important to Katie. I'm glad I could help make her day special."

The four of them fell into an uneasy silence. Abby picked at the slice of wedding cake in front of her, while Sarah turned in her seat and made a point of watching the couples on the dance floor. Chris patted the tabletop and spoke as if the past few minutes hadn't happened. "Abby, it would be a shame for you and me to come all the way to Turks and Caicos and not at least put our feet in the water. What say we take a stroll?" He pulled her to her feet, grabbing her purse and wrap as he led her out of the ballroom.

The second her feet hit the sand, Abby kicked off her sandals and breathed in as much of the salt air as her lungs would hold. The latest skirmish with Sarah left her drained. She waited while Chris tugged off his socks and shoes then rolled up his pants legs. She walked towards the surf until the waves washed over her feet.

"It's cold." Abby squealed as another wave hit then she hiked up the hem of her dress to her knees.

"What did you expect?" He chuckled then fell in beside her as she walked along the surf.

The sound of the ocean was already working its

magic. She linked arms with him. "Thanks for getting me out of there."

"What are friends for?" He cocked his head in her direction. "Tell me again why you invited that woman."

She let out a breath. Words failed her when it came to explaining how she could love someone but couldn't get along with her. "Tripp, Jessica, and Sarah are all the family Jackson and I have left."

He snorted. "You're a better person than me."

A dull ache set up in her chest. "Telling her off isn't going to change what she thinks of me. All these years later, all she sees is the nineteen-year-old who came home from New York knocked up."

Chris tugged her to a stop then took both her hands in his. "It's her loss."

It was, and Abby wasn't going to let her sister's attitude ruin another second of this day. "Didn't Katie look beautiful in her dress?"

They'd reached the end of the light from the hotel, and as they turned around Chris nodded. "I want to know how she managed to time everything so she and Jack were saying their vows at the exact moment the sun was setting."

The wind kicked up and Abby stopped to pull her wrap up around her shoulders. "You know, my favorite part was seeing Jackson's face as Katie walked to him." Tears stung her eyes. Her throat tightened as she told Chris what she'd been thinking all day. "I wish my parents had lived to see him grow up."

He passed her his handkerchief. "He's a good man. You can be proud of the job you did."

She bumped shoulders with him. Chris had come into her life at the exact moment when Jackson had needed a good man to look up to. “I had help.”

“On to your second act.” He looked back at the hotel. “I promised to help Jack organize the fireworks.”

“You go ahead. I’ll be up in a minute.”

She ambled along the water’s edge for a few minutes longer. She had time before she was expected back at the reception. Ahead she saw the shadowy outline of a man standing a few feet from the metal gate separating the hotel property from the beach. His back was turned to her but she could see the glow from his cell phone. There could be only one silhouette with such a delicious combination of broad shoulders and long legs.

A smile crossed her face as she thought about the dance she’d shared with Grant. He’d been ill at ease with the steps and no doubt not too thrilled to be dancing with a woman he didn’t know. Somehow he’d managed to turn a shortcoming into a good time. His willingness to make a fool of himself for his sister touched a chord within Abby.

She had her hand on the gate when his voice stopped her. Instead of the sensual timbre she’d enjoyed earlier, it now had an unmistakable edge. “I don’t give a flying flip what parts you need. That airplane will be ready to fly on Friday or you will be looking for a new job.”

Her opinion of him dropped a few points. Clearly, he was accustomed to having his employees do whatever it took. She hated the way people with money felt they owned those who didn’t. Not wanting to be privy to the tongue-lashing the poor employee was receiving, Abby looked around for another route. Unfortunately, the only path back to the ballroom was past him. She stepped back into the shadows and tried not to listen.

Grant paused briefly, apparently listening to his employee's defense. He spoke with a brusque tone. "If you offer a man enough money, he'll forget all about fireworks and football and get his ass to work." He paused while the person on the other end started up again, but Grant stomped on the reply. "Never mind, Jones. I'll handle this myself."

Abby heard the beep of Grant's cell phone and prayed he'd walk away so she could get back inside. Instead, he opened the gate with a flourish. "You can come out now. I'm through acting the big bad wolf."

Heat crept up her cheeks. "I'm sorry. I tried not to eavesdrop." She stepped through the gate and took her time rinsing the sand off her feet at the shower the hotel provided. She hated hearing his conversation but from the look on his face, it didn't seem to bother him. Then a thought occurred to her. "If you knew I was here, why didn't you move away?"

Grant moved in closer, cutting off her path to the ballroom. Her crossed arms signaled she hadn't been impressed with the way he'd handled his foreman. He didn't want to be a jerk but sometimes being the boss meant he had to do things he didn't enjoy. "I'm sorry you had to hear that, but I wanted to talk with you."

After their dance he'd planned to hunt her down, preferably far from anyone who'd steal her away again. Fortunately, the phone call from work had taken him outside and serendipitously put him in Abby's path.

Now he had her alone, his brain became a jumble how to convince this beautiful woman to spend time with him.

Who am I kidding? Saying she was beautiful was the greatest of understatements.

It was like saying the sea was wet. Beyond the enticing way her dress clung to her curves, he liked her confidence. "I was surprised to see you on the beach. I would have thought they'd have to drag you off the dance floor."

She looked over her shoulder at the water. "With all the wedding preparations, I've barely gotten to see the water much less get in it."

Grant's brain kicked into hyper-drive. Now he knew how to get her to stay. "You like the water?" He envisioned a long weekend on the beach with her.

"Love it. I've only ever been to Jekyll Island and the Gulf Coast, but nothing spells vacation like my toes in the water and my butt in the sand." She laughed as she said it, her voice sounding like ice cubes in a glass of twelve-year-old scotch.

"I have an idea. Why don't you go diving with me tomorrow?" He bet she'd look good in a bikini.

Her eyes grew wide and she took a step backward. "Thank you, but I'd be too terrified to do that."

He wasn't ready to admit defeat. Once he made up his mind, he stuck it through to the end. He'd made up his mind about Abby. "I'm a dive master. I could teach you. It's only fair since you shared something you're good at. You have to give me a chance to play teacher and you be the student." He wasn't above playing dirty to get what he wanted.

"I have to leave in the morning." She dropped her gaze and edged her way around him.

He touched her arm. "No, you don't. School doesn't start again until Monday."

Her head shot up, eyes wide with surprise.

He knew she was a teacher because Katie cited her future mother-in-law as the reason she'd changed her major to education halfway through her sophomore year. He guessed school would resume on the first Monday after the New Year.

"I bought a ticket on Caribbean Air, no changes allowed."

"You can fly back with me on my plane. Since Katie and Jack won't be coming back for another week, there will be room." The whole thing made perfect sense to him, a couple of extra days in the sun for him to wine and dine his way into her good graces. Nothing was more convincing than a fancy hotel and private jet.

She cocked her head at him and her fists hit her hips. "Are you one of those people who think if everyone did things his way the world would be perfect?"

Grant abandoned his persuasion with money strategy. Perhaps a little honesty would work. "Yes, I am. I'm sorry if I came off pushy. I only wanted to be sure you had a good time while you were here."

She fixed him with a glare even the near darkness couldn't hide. "I was having a good time until a second ago."

He had one more trick up his sleeve. If this didn't work, he'd admit he was out of his league with this woman. "Then would you do one thing?"

Chapter Three

God, she was such a sucker for blue eyes. His sparkled and danced enticing her to comply. As if that weren't enough, his dark hair and Roman nose reminded her of what she thought Aries would have looked like: a beautiful warrior who was accustomed to getting his way.

He continued, putting more than a touch of persuasion in his voice. "I promise I won't ask for anything else. You won't even have to speak to me the next time our families get together."

Abby remembered she'd have to see him every holiday now they were related so it was probably a good idea to make nice. She still didn't trust him. He switched personas too easily: paternal with Katie, a taskmaster with his employee, and charming with her.

"What?" The suspicion arose similar to when a student tried to hand her something he'd picked up on the playground. Twenty years of experience had shown her it was usually something she wouldn't like.

"I want to finish our dance. I had a really cool spin I was planning for our finale I didn't get to do."

The man was good. Not only did he offer her something she couldn't resist, he threw in a measure of guilt to boot—and didn't wait for her to agree but pulled her to him.

She opened her mouth to point out there wasn't any

music but the French doors leading to the ballroom opened and music from the reception flooded the patio. If she believed in magic, she'd swear he'd willed the unfolding events. Everyone and everything around him seemed to bend to his will.

His smile revealed a pair of dimples. "Perfect."

He moved the two of them in a small circle, not exactly dancing as much as swaying in time with the music. Then he started humming, a low rumble she couldn't help but feel since he was holding her to his chest. His hearing must have been better than hers since she couldn't make out the song. Then again the sound of blood thrumming in her ears drowned out everything else.

After a moment, her heartbeat settled. This was lovely, almost perfect, as he'd declared. Between the sound of the surf and the breeze caressing her neck she let her body relax. Perhaps this was more innocent than she thought. She'd let herself become jaded in the last few years. Not everyone was trying to pull something. He was being nice. "I'm sorry I was rude earlier."

He looked down at her, his brows arched. "Does this mean you've changed your mind?"

"I didn't want to seem ungrateful. You've been so generous already." Abby owed him an explanation. "Even talking about scuba diving makes my palms sweat."

She spent so many years being cautious that the idea of doing anything adventurous seemed foreign. Neither did she want to be in his debt. She valued her independence more than anything.

"Don't apologize. I like that you stood up for yourself. Katie tells me I can be a bulldozer. It does my ego good to be told 'no' once in a while." He resumed swaying and humming.

It felt good to clear the air. She didn't want to do anything to make things awkward between them.

Abby wasn't good at keeping up polite conversation, but he didn't fill the silence with chatter either. Within seconds her mind wandered down another rabbit trail: luggage to pack, early morning flight to catch, thank you notes to write.

When Grant took a step she wasn't ready for, his thigh brushed hard against her. The friction burned through her, bringing her back to the here and now and awakened dormant parts of her body. She jerked back to give them some space. The last thing she needed was for him to realize what the contact had done to her. Unfortunately, when she stepped back her heel caught the edge of the pool. "Crap!" She teetered, unable to regain her balance.

Grant pulled her to him. "Sorry. I didn't realize we had gotten so close."

Deftly, he moved them away from the edge. If he noticed her embarrassment or could feel the heat radiating off her body, he was gentleman enough to hide it. He moved them to the shadows which was a good thing because he couldn't see the pink which had bloomed from her neck to her ears.

The bad thing was the darkness only made her more aware of how good his arms felt around her. It took every ounce of self-control to keep her hand resting lightly on his upper arm where it belonged because her fingers itched to take in the strength, to let her hand trail down his arm. The laws of attraction were hard at work making her want what she shouldn't have.

When the song ended, he stopped moving but didn't let her go. She tried to ease herself out of his embrace. He only drew her in closer so their bodies connected from her cheek resting on his chest to his hips meeting the soft part of her belly.

"The song is over," she whispered.

His hand skimmed over her bare back sending shivers down her spine. "I know."

"You can let go."

Instead, he kissed her. Lips soft as suede brushed against hers, moving tentatively. Cologne filled her head with its delicious sandalwood scent. His body warmed her to the bone. Abby's hand moved to his neck and brought him down hard against her lips. When his tongue begged entrance, she opened and let him explore her mouth hungrily. He tasted of whisky and something wonderfully spicy.

The sound of laughter brought her back to reality and threw cold water on her lust even better than the pool could have. Any number of wedding guests could have strolled by to see her making a fool of herself. Abby broke away, rushing blindly towards the hotel.

Grant was on her before she got two steps away, pulling her to a stop. "Wait." The lights showed on his face, revealing hooded eyelids and the scowl of a warrior.

She had to get away. Not because she feared what he would do to her but what she wanted him to do. She couldn't trust her self-control to stand there and explain. She shoved him away as if her life depended on it.

Her fear had given her physical if not moral strength. He took a step back. Then she saw what lay behind him. In slow motion she watched his arms pinwheel. She reached out to him and their fingers connected for the briefest second before he slipped from her grasp. Abby watched behind splayed fingers as he fell backward into the water.

By the time she was kneeling at the edge he was breaking the surface. He gasped for air. “Oh God, I’m so sorry.”

She extended her hand, part help and part peace offering. Instead, he planted his palms against the pool’s apron and catapulted himself out of the water. She scrambled to her feet in time to see him fishing a phone from his pocket.

“I’ll pay to replace it.” More a plea than a promise.

He stared at the thing in his palm as if willing it back to life before running his hand over his scalp. She should have looked for a towel to give him, apologized again, something to make the situation better.

Then he burst out laughing, a deep masculine rumble she would have enjoyed under better circumstances. “I didn’t see that one coming.”

She wrapped her arms around her waist and took a step back. “Again, I’m so sorry. I’ve never…” *wanted someone so much...* “overreacted like that.”

He shoved the phone in his pocket and placed his hand on her arm. Even in the dim light she could see the sincerity in the depths of his blue eyes. “It’s me who needs to apologize. Obviously, I overstepped my bounds.”

She hated him shouldering the blame since she’d wanted the kiss as much as he did. But, admitting as much would only lead him to think she was a cougar who routinely prowled weddings. She extended her hand to him and offered him a smile she didn't quite feel. "Let's chalk it up to the romantic atmosphere."

As he took the hand she offered, he didn't seem so sure. "That's probably what it was." He looked over his shoulder at the hotel then down at his clothes. "Everyone should be coming out in a few minutes for the fireworks. I guess I need to make myself scarce."

She took a step towards the hotel. "If anyone asks, I'll tell them you needed to take a phone call from work." The fib pricked her conscience because he wouldn't be taking any calls from his office thanks to her. Once she got back home, she'd have to find a way to make things right with him.

After slipping through the French doors, she took a minute to pull herself together. Just because her insides were in a knot, didn't mean she wanted to look like a hot mess. She ran her trembling fingers over her hair. Only a hairspray-defying curl had gone astray, and she quickly tucked it behind her ear. Her hopes of blending in with the other guests were obliterated when she looked down. The front of her dress was completely soaked.

She considered returning to her suite but she'd miss the fireworks and bouquet toss. It might not be the most important part of the wedding, but Katie had made a point of asking Abby to be there. She took a deep breath and opened the door.

With the reception ending, the lights of the ballroom had been raised. To her relief the remaining guests were focused on the main door where the bride and groom would make their final appearance. A gaggle of bridesmaids and Katie's other single friends were waiting for the bride to throw her bouquet.

Fleetingly, it dawned on Abby her new daughter-in-law might have been planning to throw her the bouquet.

The idea of getting married might have been laughable if her mistakes with men weren't so unfortunate. She couldn't even manage a simple dance without turning it into a disaster. She eased around the perimeter of the room hoping not to be noticed by the other guests.

"Where have you been?"

She jumped at the sound of Chris' voice. His gazed slipped from her face down to her dress and back again. "What happened?"

"A wave got me." Which was mostly true. Except the wave hadn't been the ocean or even the splash from the pool. She'd been caught up in a tsunami named Grant Davis.

Chapter Four

"Right here's fine."

Abby leapt from the backseat of the taxi while it was still moving. She met the poor fellow who was huffing and puffing to keep up with her pace by the trunk and thrust the fare and tip into his hand. Taking her suitcase in one hand and the garment bag in the other, she strode to the automatic doors of the airport. Finally, the knot that had been sitting in her stomach since Grant kissed her began to untangle.

When she reached the check-in desk, not a single light was on, nor a person visible. She checked her watch, three hours until her flight left.

What was wrong with these airlines? Didn't they know how desperately I need off this island?

She scanned the lobby hoping to see someone dressed in the bright blue and green uniforms of Caribbean Air. She'd talk whoever she could find into letting her check in early.

Suddenly the message board blinked to life. As the announcement scrolled past, the knot returned. Her airline, the one from which she'd purchased a nonrefundable, nontransferable ticket back to Atlanta, had gone bankrupt and folded last night.

I can fix this.

She scooted over to another line feeling hopeful again. It was the hometown carrier and surely they could come up with a solution. When her turn came, she put on her best "please help me" smile and approached the ticket agent.

Twenty minutes and a couple, "I'm sorry that's the best I can do," replies from the agent and she was left with two choices. She could borrow a thousand dollars from Chris or see if Turks and Caicos needed any special education teachers. She thanked the agent and stepped aside to make the call.

As she drew her phone from her purse, she formulated a plan to pay back her friend. It was only until she could cash in one of her savings bonds. Unfortunately, that meant she wouldn't be remodeling the bathroom this year. Oh well, another year in the 1930s wouldn't kill her. She reminded herself how much she liked the white porcelain fixtures and nickel faucets.

She was about to push the Send button when out of the corner of her eye she caught someone approaching. She turned to face the last person she expected or wanted to see. Grant had on perfectly worn jeans, snug white T-shirt, and a pair of aviator sunglasses that reminded her of a taller, better-looking version of Tom Cruise in *Top Gun*. To top it off he was sporting an ear-to-ear grin.

Why does his smile always make me think he was up to mischief?

"Hi." He thrust the blue silk wrap and matching purse she'd worn to the wedding towards her. "You left these by the pool last night."

She took her things, tucking them in her carry-on. "You didn't have to come all the way here just for that."

Grant took a step closer, eyeing all five and a half feet of her. "I heard about Caribbean Air and came because I want to offer you something."

He was close enough she could catch a whiff of his aftershave. Her pulse kicked up a notch as she breathed in the spicy scent. "What?"

"If you agree, we can consider it a repayment for the phone you drowned." His voice held a trace of humor.

He'd known her less than a day, but he'd had already honed in on her sense of honor. "Go ahead."

He wrapped his hand around the handle of her suitcase. "I have to head to Atlanta and I'd like you to keep me company on the way back."

Decision time. Shell out money she couldn't afford or spend three hours with a man who impaired her judgment in a way alcohol never could. He stepped closer so the hard muscles of his chest were all she could see. Abby swallowed.

"You certainly know how to work a girl's rock-and-hard-place dilemma to your advantage."

His eyes nailed into her. "I most certainly do."

Dear Lord, what am I about to do?

"All right, I'm in."

Before she could rethink her decision, he'd snagged her luggage and was wheeling it away from the check-in desk. The man moved like a cheetah on a mission, and even her long legs had to trot to keep up. She paused at a set of double doors marked: chartered departures. Nervous anticipation had her heart keeping a staccato beat. People in her world rarely traveled outside The States, and they never chartered their own planes.

"Got your passport handy?" His broad grin suggested they were embarking on a grand adventure. She envied him his laisser-faire take on life. He didn't even seem bothered by their kiss last night. Or the aftermath. Well, she'd just have to take a page from his playbook. If he could act like their kiss had never happened, she could too.

She dug in her purse and extracted the blue booklet, waving it for him to see. "Right here."

Grant nodded a quick response and led her to the custom's queue. While waiting their turn, Abby stole sideways glances at him. The snug fitting T-shirt and jeans he wore looked every bit as good on him as the tux had. Better in fact since it looked more like him than the suit. From the corner of her eye she saw a day's growth of beard shadow his jaw, softening its hard edge. Her fingers itched to run over the whiskers, to feel their roughness.

The problem with pretending nothing had happened was not only had something happened, it continued to happen. She was attracted to him. Not in a "wow, that's a good-looking man" kind a way, but in a way that made her feel as if she was losing control. At least there'd be other passengers to distract her.

She'd been so lost in her own thoughts, the customs and immigration process passed with barely a blip on her radar screen. Once again she was trailing along behind him as his long legs chewed up the carpet. He paused at a set of glass doors, holding them open for her. "Plane's this way."

Then they were out in the bright light and warm breeze of the Caribbean. If it weren't for her constant worry of doing something inappropriate with him, the experience might have been fun.

A line of twin engine planes edging the runway brought her crashing back to reality. These machines were too small to send out over the open ocean. In fact, she'd driven bigger cars. Abby could feel the icy prick of anxiety climb up her spine and take root in her soul.

Talk about jumping from the frying pan and into the fire. Where was a tranquilizer when she needed one? One thing about the situation, if she was worried about dying, she wouldn't be thinking about kissing Grant again.

As he neared one of the larger examples of the flying death machines, she noticed a small smile creep to the corners of his mouth. This wasn't simply another machine to him. This was his baby. The tri colors, white, gold, and black, gave the jet a sleek, majestic edge the white and primary colored planes lacked. She liked it based solely on the fact it looked big enough to stay aloft for several hundred miles.

Grant left her side and began examining one of the wings. The way he ran his hands over the edge was more than pride of ownership; he examined it as if it were a racehorse headed to the track. "Doesn't the pilot usually do that?"

"He does." Another impish grin creased his face.

Embarrassment flooded her cheeks. She hadn't meant to sound like a know-it-all, but thankfully he didn't seem to take offense at her question. If fact, between the inspection he was giving his baby and the way he kept looking back at her, he seemed to be having the time of his life.

She was doing all right herself. The news he'd be piloting the plane settled her nerves. If he was in the cockpit and she was in the cabin, perhaps she could make it through the flight without doing something idiotic.

While he performed his pre-flight, she performed a little subtle observation of her own. From the moment he moved from her side, his full focus was on the plane. From nose to tail nothing escaped his scrutiny. She knew what the plane must be feeling. Every time he looked at her it was as if he could see her every nuance. Perhaps knowing he'd looked her over and like what he saw was what caused her to behave so impulsively. No, she corrected herself. She'd never pushed the blame for her actions on to others before, and she wasn't going to start now.

Finally, after he'd crawled under the plane's belly and even kicked the tires, he circled back to her. "She's ready to go." He scooped up their luggage.

They moved to the door of the plane and stopped. His arms were full, but the thoughts of opening the door had her arms frozen by her side. Not only because she might break something, but once the door was open there was no going back.

"Just pop the latch and the door will open." Anticipation colored his voice. For him taking to the air was a wonderful excitement, not the dooms day experience she was making this out to be.

Shaking herself mentally, she reached out and pulled the lever. The door seemed to come alive under her hand. It swung free and the steps descended into place smoothly.

"Better let me go in first." He nudged her hip with his.

"Sorry." She moved aside, feeling a little stupid to

have been standing in the way while he had an armload of bags.

She followed him up the stairs and got an eye-full of how the rich and famous traveled. Leather covered every surface that wasn't done in burl wood or chrome.

LED lights twinkled from above giving the cabin the look of a luxury spaceship. She took several breaths to calm her nerves. It even had that new car smell. "Wow," she whispered. "It's the most beautiful thing I've ever been in."

He stowed their luggage in an overhead compartment and turned to her. "Thanks." Then he pointed to a small galley lined with crystal barware. "Can I offer you a diet soda or bottled water?"

"I'm good." She continued to take in the well-appointed interior. To her right were six empty recliner-sized chairs. "Where are the other passengers sitting? I don't want to take your mom's seat or anything."

He shook his head and shot her a lopsided grin that revealed a dimple. "It's just us." He thumbed in the direction of the cockpit. "You're sitting up front to keep me company."

What the heck?

Abby blinked a couple times while her brain played catch up. Three hours hemmed in with Fly Boy. But at this point what could she do? With a glance heavenward, she followed him as he inched his way through the small port and into the cockpit.

Even through her dismay at the situation she'd gotten herself into, she couldn't help but notice how he nimbly contorted his body to fit in the tight quarters. This was a man who knew how to make his body do what he wanted it to.

Abby followed his example and eased her way into the co-pilot's seat. Her eyes grew wide as she saw a bank of instruments and yoke a mere two inches from her lap. She wouldn't have to worry about keeping her hands-off Grant. She'd be trying to not touch the instruments. Abby tucked her hands under her legs.

Grant reached over to pat her knee. "Relax. This will be the ride of your life."

His words weren't making her feel any better. One wrong move and it would all be over. "What if I touch something?" Her voice rose an octave.

"Don't worry so much. Relax and enjoy the ride." Still grinning, he eased over her body. His eyes bored into hers and his lips were no more than an inch from where they'd been last night. She could even feel the heat radiating off his skin and smell his aftershave. She tensed, waiting for him to kiss her again. His hands moved forward, and she licked her lips.

"Here, let me fasten your seatbelt for you."

She bit back a groan. Forget something for anxiety, she needed a pill to curb her overactive imagination. Abby folded her hands in her lap and resolved to at least try to act normal.

He tightened her seatbelt without seeming to notice her faux pas then turned to push up a switch guard and flipped a lever. "Let's wake this baby up."

Abby watched as he fired up the machine. After a few seconds, curiosity about the switches, dials, and the artificial horizon overtook her embarrassment. When he put on his head set and pointed to its mate draped over the yoke in front of her, she quickly put it on, excited to hear what he'd tell her.

"This is your captain speaking." His voice came

alive in her ear. "We'll be departing the gate in a few minutes, but first I'd like to go over a few safety features. We'll be flying over water for most of the flight and in the unlikely event of a water landing…you're completely screwed."

Abby shoved her fists over her eyes as scenes from one of those old airport disaster movies flashed through her head. There was no way she could take three minutes much less three hours in this aluminum death trap. Her hands trembled as she snatched at the harness. She'd get out of here and take her chances on a real plane.

His hand on her bare arm stilled her. "I'm sorry." The amusement bled from his voice. "I was just trying to be funny."

She cracked her eyes to see if he were making fun of her. Someone like Grant wasn't afraid of anything. The world was one big adventure. And people like that rarely understood the fear of others.

Instead of mockery she saw compassion tinged with embarrassment. "I'm such a jerk." His palm slid down her arm and squeezed her hand. "Nothing bad is going to happen to us. I promise."

Still too scared to speak, she could only acknowledge his words with a nod. She took several deep breaths and willed her legs to stop trembling. Eventually her heart rate settled to double digits and she turned her attention to the view ahead.

The next several minutes were a rush of garbled instructions from the tower and a series of turns. Then before she realized what was happening, they were barreling down the runway and into the sky.

The sensation of gravity pressing her into the seat

caused another wave of fear. She squeezed her eyes shut. "Let me know when it's over."

Her heart pounded in her chest until she thought if she looked down her T-shirt would be stained red.

"Look. Last chance to see the island."

She couldn't let fear keep her from a last glimpse of azure-blue ocean. She cracked her lids as Grant banked the airplane, giving her a wide view. She pressed her hand to the window. "I can almost feel the warmth coming off the waves."

A chuckle brought her attention to him. "I can't believe I couldn't convince you to dive with me. Clearly, you have a thing for the water."

His expression stunned her. Passion, joy, and lust for living shown in his blue eyes. He held her gaze for a pair of heartbeats then turned his attention back to flying. Now that was something she could really fall into.

Grant leveled off the jet at thirty-thousand feet and engaged the autopilot. Now that the plane wasn't taking up all his attention, he shot Abby a furtive glance to be sure his stupid remarks earlier weren't still worrying her.

She'd gone from clutching the seat to resting her hands in her lap and although she was watching out the windscreen ahead, she didn't look exactly relaxed. She did however look hot as hell. Her black T-shirt accentuated her fair skin, and the scooped neckline showed off her collar bones and just a hint of cleavage.

Sensing he'd been eyeballing her, her gaze briefly touched on him before hurrying away. Three hours of strained silence and awkward looks were going to feel like an eternity. "Talk to me. You're supposed to be keeping me company."

She turned to him and a beautiful blush colored her cheeks. "Sorry. I didn't want to distract you while you were flying the plane."

He patted the glare shield. "Autopilot. While I can't go to the galley and fix you a sandwich, I'm all yours until time to land."

She stared at her hands, lacing and unlacing them. Then she cocked her head. "How long have you been a pilot?"

"Since I was old enough to climb behind the yoke. Why are you worried I'll crash?"

The blush bloomed upward to her hairline. "Just wondering what got you interested in aviation."

Though he was proud of how he'd turned his father's business into a success, he didn't want to talk about himself. That conversation could be summed up in one sentence: good in business, sucked at relationships. "Tell me about yourself. What drives you to get out of bed in the morning?"

The fire he'd noticed in her eyes yesterday was back. "My students. I love when the light bulb goes off."

School, not one of his favorite topics of conversation. But listening to her excited voice was like rain on dry earth. He had to keep her talking. "My sister said you were a professional dancer. How long were you in New York?"

Her laugh sounded like bells. "Katie was being generous. My dancing career lasted about a year."

"Did something go wrong like an injury to make you stop?"

She dropped her gaze. "Something like that."

A memory played of Abby's confident, joyous expression as she danced. "Must be tough. I'd hate it if I couldn't do what I love."

She shrugged. "I adjusted. Besides being a professional dancer doesn't lend itself to single parenting." Her hand rested on his knee for a moment. "Don't get me wrong, I love teaching. My students keep me on my toes like ballet never could."

He barked a laugh. "I hated school. Every minute of every day was shear torture, and I'm sure I was no picnic for the teachers either."

She bit her lip as if she were holding back her words. After a pair of seconds, a giggle escaped her mouth. "Somehow, I don't find it hard to believe you were a challenge in the classroom, what with your dominant personality and adventurous spirit and all."

Her hand found its way back to his leg again, sending a shockwave of desire up his spine. "Lest you think I was the ideal student, I'll let you in on a little secret." She lowered her voice. "I hated school too. I didn't learn to read until the third grade. That's why I decided to go into teaching. I wanted to work with kids for whom school wasn't the happy place."

Grant stared at Abby slack-jawed and mute. When he'd offered her his plane, he'd just been hoping for a short, playful diversion. Maybe a kiss at the end to see if he got the same tingle as he had last night. He never expected she'd bowl him over. No wonder his sister wanted to emulate her. She was the real deal, purpose driven, smart as hell, and so sensual. If it weren't for the yoke hemming him in and the fact she probably didn't want him to, he'd take her in his arms and kiss her blind. "Wow! Woman, you take my breath away."

Chapter Five

With a screech of tires against concrete, Grant landed the jet back in the real world. Most of his attention was trained on slowing six tons of metal below a hundred miles an hour, but his ears picked up on a sudden escape of breath from Abby's lungs. "I think I like taking off better than I like landing."

After negotiating onto the taxiway, he reached over to give her knee a friendly squeeze. "Come on, it wasn't that bad."

She let out another one of her musical laughs. "I have to admit this trip was actually all right."

From his end, it had been fantastic. Once she'd finally relaxed, she'd taken the job of keeping him company to heart. His abs ached from laughing as she'd entertained him with stories about her students. The news his brother-in-law, Jack, had played in an indie-rock band in high school was fodder for future ribbing.

Grant steered the plane past the commercial gates to the fixed base operation side of Hartsfield-Jackson airport, parking it in the space he leased. "I have a car on this side of the airport. I'd be happy to drive you over to long-term parking."

Abby unfastened her seatbelt. "You've already done so much. I'm sure I can manage to get back to my car."

He didn't doubt for a minute she was perfectly

capable of negotiating immigration and hailing a taxi. After hearing her explain how she had remodeled her home, he didn't think there was anything she couldn't do for herself.

Following her example with the seatbelt, he then put the plane to bed before leading the way out of the cockpit. While she donned her sunglasses, he retrieved their luggage and released the latch on the plane's door. Once they were on the tarmac, he put his plan into motion. "Why don't we first stop off at a coffee shop for some breakfast then we'll find your car."

She reached for the handle of her suitcase and offered him a small smile. "That's very kind, but I have about a million things I need to do before school starts back on Monday." Then she pulled her phone out of her purse. "It's okay to use this now, right? I want to let my friend, Chris, know I made it home okay. He'll be worried when he hears about Caribbean Air."

Her words brought him up short. After they'd parted ways last night, he hung around in the shadows wanting to see his sister off. In addition to fireworks, he'd gotten a view of Abby wrapped up in some guy's arms. She wasn't married and assumed at the time the guy was a relative.

Maybe this Chris fellow was a friend with a benefits package. The thought turned his stomach. Having been on the receiving end of infidelity, fooling around with another man's woman was a hard limit for him.

Still it always paid to get the facts straight. "Why wasn't he on the same flight as you?"

She began texting while she explained. "He's flying up to Charleston to meet with a potential client.

He does restorations on old homes and is hoping to get the contract to remodel an antebellum down there."

"Sounds interesting." The way she'd handled herself made him think she was a straight shooter, not the type to fool around. But what did he know? He'd never thought his ex, Heather, was capable of cheating either. "So how long have you and Chris been a couple?"

She looked up from her phone and blinked a couple times. "We're not. Why do you ask?"

"I like to have all the players in a situation accounted for."

Abby lowered her sunglasses so he could see her whisky-colored eyes. "I think I need to reiterate what I said last night. That kiss was a 'one off' and won't be repeated. And once again I apologize if I have given you any indication I wanted more."

Water off a duck's butt.

Grant smiled to himself. Her mouth might be saying, "She's just not that into you," but the pulse thrumming in her neck and the heat radiating from her eyes were screaming otherwise. Grant closed the distance between them, wanting to kiss the lies right off her lips. Instead, he grinned. "Message received and understood."

Immediately he backed away and let her head for the FBO gate. His gaze trailed after her as she walked past the guard station and turned left towards a line of taxis. "Go ahead, beautiful lady." He was no stranger to a challenge. In fact, he was on a first name basis with struggle and fighting for what he wanted was second nature. "Play like you're not interested because it will only make your surrender sweeter."

Chapter Six

Grant ran his hand along the skin of the plane. The way she laid all open with the engine cowl off and the nosecone removed made him think of a patient in surgery. “She’s going to be back in the air by Friday, right.” He had to shout over the whine of a sheet metal grinder on the other side of the hanger. The mechanic Grant had been grilling pulled his hand out of the engine long enough to shoot the boss a thumbs up.

With that Grant wandered off. He was procrastinating plain and simple, just like he’d done when he was back in school. Anything to get out of sitting behind a desk all day. He eased over to another of his planes and fisted a wrench from a nearby toolbox. “Are you servicing the landing gear or the tires?”

A gray-haired man pulled his head out of the wheel well. “Tires, they’re due for maintenance.”

Grant nodded at Andy Foster, one of a couple go-to guys who’d been around since before the earth cooled.

“Well then, I’ll leave you to it.”

“Mr. Davis,” Andy called after Grant turned to leave.

He couldn’t get used to people with forty years on him and a ton more experience calling him by his old man’s name. “S’up?”

“Thanks for the overtime.”

Grant shook his head. "No man, thank you for bailing me out. We'd have lost that account if you hadn't gotten that engine installed on time."

The guy grinned. "Can't say no to double-holiday pay."

Andy's wife had finished radiation for breast cancer back in the fall. God only knew how much the man owed in hospital bills. Grant had offered to cover the out of pocket expenses, but Andy wouldn't hear of it. As a compromise Grant had been sending all the overtime his way.

"How's the wife doing?"

The guy suddenly became interested in a spot of grease on the floor, toeing it with his boot. "She was real sick between Christmas and New Year's. She caught something from one of the grandkids and ended up spending a week in the hospital." The guy's face shot up, pegging Grant with a haunted look. "Thinking we might lose her to something like pneumonia after she'd survived cancer scared me to death."

"I'm sorry to hear that." Grant took a step back, feeling uncomfortable with the anguish in the guy's voice. "Let me or Maggie know if there's anything we can do, or if you need to take some personal leave." Grant turned to leave.

"One more thing."

When Grant turned to look at the man, the hard set to his jaw spoke of a decision made. "I've worked since I was fifteen years old. Every hour I spent away from the job, I felt was a wasted opportunity to be making money for my family. Seeing her in ICU changed that. I'm gonna retire at the end of the month."

That was the last thing Grant ever expected to hear

come out of Andy's mouth. He'd have bet a week's pay the guy would retire when they hauled him out of there with a toe tag. "I'm sorry to hear that, but I understand."

At one point in his life, Grant thought the best thing he could do for his family was to make money. That belief cost him his marriage, so yeah, he totally understood. Andy jerked his chin in a nod then turned back to his work, and Grant quit procrastinating.

An hour later a sharp rap on the door of Grant's office brought his head up from the computer screen. "Thank goodness." He welcomed the interruption. The headache coupled with his gnat sized attention span weren't making getting the FAA certification he'd been working on any easier. Forget wrapping his bike around an oak tree or having a parachute failure, the paper pushers who ran the three letter agencies were going to be the death of him.

"Come on in, Maggie."

She popped the door handle and backed in the room with a stack of papers under her arm and two cups of coffee balanced in her hand. She passed him one then plopped down in the chair across the metal desk from him. "Here's the stuff you need to look at." She slid the papers over. "I've highlighted the important sections and flagged where you need to sign. They're all standard charter contracts, nothing funky."

Grant flipped through the pages and once he'd signed in all the right spots, he slid them back to her. "Before I forget, Katie sent you these." He passed her a manila envelope.

Pulling out several photos taken at the wedding, she smiled. "She didn't have to do that." She glanced up at Grant. "The kids and I had a great time at the wedding."

Grant leaned over, smiling at the photo of two cute kids flanking the bride. "I'm glad you enjoyed it. Lexi did a great job as flower girl."

Maggie offered up one of her good-natured chuckles. "She insisted on wearing the dress to school that next Monday, and Matt was proud of his sunburn." She sent him a gentle smile. "The trip made getting through the holidays without Brian a lot easier."

He nodded. "I told him I would look after y'all while he was in Afghanistan and a little R and R is the least I could do. By the way, when was the last time you heard from him?"

Maggie beamed at the mention of her older brother. "We video-chatted last night. He said to tell you he got the box of cigars."

"There's more where that came from. Tell him to let me know if he wants anything else."

"Will do. Don't forget the CPA's coming tomorrow."

Grant dug his fists into his eyes. The mere mention of one more three-letter demon was enough to send his headache to DEF-CON two. "I won't forget."

Having succeeded in keeping Grant on the straight and narrow for another day, she snagged the collection of photos as she got up from her seat. She glanced back over her shoulder on her way out. "There was one thing Brian said he'd like."

Her mischievous grin confused him. "Sure. Tell me what he wants, and I'll take care of it."

Her voice had a teasing lilt. "He'd like an eight by ten of you on the dance floor. When I told him you did a waltz and a foxtrot at Katie's wedding, he didn't believe me."

"Whatever." He shook his head.

I'm going to be a hundred before I live those dances down.

Still chuckling, he settled back into his chair and gave the paperwork another shot. His good mood didn't last long. After a few minutes, the words began to blur together and the thrumming in his head picked up tempo.

He reached in his desk for a bottle of pain reliever and washed down two tablets with the dregs of the coffee Maggie had brought him. Maybe he needed glasses or a day off. Other than when it was his time to take care of Grace, he hadn't been anywhere other than the hanger since… Jeez, it had been the wedding.

Matt and Lexi weren't the only ones who'd had a good time at the beach. Along with sand and water, the memory of creamy skin, whisky-colored eyes, and golden curls came rushing back. If he started thinking about Abby, he'd be at his desk until he was drawing Social Security.

Placing his palms against his head, he adjusted the kink in his neck and redoubled his efforts to plow through the bureaucratic bull. His determination lasted about ten minutes before he found his mind drifting back to Abby. She'd been the most exciting thing he'd come up against in a long time, and he jumped out of perfectly good airplanes for kicks and giggles. He just had a couple problems to overcome in his plan to woo the lovely Ms. Roberts. The mile-high brick wall she kept around herself and his freakishly long work week.

Once he started thinking about her, he had as much

chance finishing the paperwork as he did learning to dance. He let out a groan. "I gotta get out of here."

He blasted past Maggie's desk. "I've got an errand to run. I'll be back in the morning." He hit the push bar on the door leading to the hanger and breathed in the smell of jet fuel and metal. Not as enticing as the perfume he remembered Abby wearing, but a close second.

****

"What do you think of this picture?" Katie clicked the mouse to enlarge the next wedding photo. She'd invited Abby and Chris to her mother's house to select wedding pictures.

After a formal dinner, complete with crystal and china, they'd been seated in a great room that felt more like it belonged in a British TV drama than a home in the prestigious suburbs of north Atlanta.

Out of the hundred or so they'd already viewed, Abby had yet to find one where the couple didn't look like they belonged on the pages of a bridal magazine. "That's a good one as well."

"It's too artistic for my taste." From the opposite sofa, Katherine Davis scratched a line through the list the photographer had provided.

Abby eyed the black and white shot, and then her daughter-in-law who looked a little hurt at her mother's remarks.

"Well, I like it. It looks like something out of Hollywood's heyday." Then she turned to draw Jackson and Chris into the conversation. "What do you guys think?"

"Whatever makes you ladies happy is fine with me." Jackson barely turned his attention from the laptop mirroring the one the women were using. He and Chris had hung in there for the first fifty or so pictures before Jackson pulled out his machine and the two guys got busy working on their fantasy football teams. Much to Katherine's displeasure.

It looked like the bride was fine without her new husband's input, however. She blew Jackson a kiss across the table and chuckled. "Good answer, good answer," she sing-songed while clapping. Then she touched Abby's hand. "Here's something you missed." She pointed to a photo of the bouquet toss.

Abby hadn't exactly missed the melee of single girls grappling for the prize. Her mind replayed the pool-side scene that led up to her very wet reason for staying in the shadows.

Katie bumped shoulders with Abby. "Doesn't matter." Her eyes snapped with mischief. "You'll get a guy, even without the good luck charm."

Abby choked on her after dinner wine. "You think because you're happy the whole world should be paired up."

"Yep, I do." She gestured to Chris. You too, we need to find you a man as well."

Abby's best friend looked up from his laptop. "From your lips to cupid's ears."

Katherine stiffened. "Let's see another, darling."

With the click of the mouse, the oversized screen was filled with a face Abby had been trying to forget.

Katie touched the screen. "This is one of my favorites." Affection infused her words. "Don't you think that's a good one of Grant and you dancing?"

Abby allowed herself to linger on his features for a second before she looked away. She didn't need to see a photo to remember that straight shot of jaw punctuated by the deepest cleft she'd ever seen or blue eyes so piercing he'd seen to her soul.

"It's very nice." Her response came out thin and reedy. She held her breath, hoping she'd been the only one to notice the quiver in her voice.

Thank goodness, Katie was in bridal nirvana and oblivious to Abby's reaction. "Well, I think you ought to have a copy in your album."

Abby took a deep breath and prayed for calm. "I have enough pictures with me in them. Besides, I've reached the outer edges of my budget."

Yeah, the last thing she wanted to pay money for was a reminder of what had happened to her common sense. Now *she* was the one wanting to steer the conversation to another subject. "Katherine, how have you been keeping yourself busy now that the big event is over?"

From her perch on the opposite side of her daughter, she gestured grandly as the group's attention diverted to her. "I've been planning a trip to…"

The door leading to the kitchen opened, stopping Katherine mid-answer.

And freezing Abby in her seat.

"I heard there was a party going on over here." Grant used those long legs of his to cross the huge room in a couple strides. As he bent to give his mother and sister each a peck on the cheek, his gaze stayed locked on Abby.

Then he walked around the coffee table and sat next to her on the large sofa.

The warm scent of his aftershave filled her head, turning her insides all gooey. Well, that blew that theory out of the water. Over the past three weeks she'd convinced herself the attraction was due to the romantic vibes saturating the island air.

"Are you hungry?" Katherine cooed. "There's plenty filet mignon left."

Grant stretched his arm over the back of the sofa, further invading Abby's personal space. "I've eaten, Mother, but thanks. I just dropped by for a moment on the way home."

"Let me get you some dessert."

As Katherine scooted to the kitchen, Grant leaned in. "Push anyone into the pool lately?" His breath tickled her ear, sending a tendril of heat licking down her spine.

"No." She choked out the word, checking the room to see who might have heard. When she saw the others were absorbed in their respective laptops, she shot back a snark of her own. "Scare anyone with your safety briefing?"

"You're the only one." He flashed a grin. Then his hand brushed across her hair, sending her pulse into triple digits.

Katherine breezed back into the room. "I was just going to tell Abby about my trip to Aspen."

Abby jolted as the timely interruption snatched her from thoughts of how good his hands would feel on her. "Please do." She slid over, putting some space between Grant and her. "It sounds wonderful."

Katherine launched into a detailed description of her trip Abby barely heard. From the corner of her eye, she watched as Grant brought forkfuls of cake to his mouth.

Lucky cake.

When Katherine finished outlining her itinerary, he laid the plate on the coffee table, wiping his mouth with the linen napkin. "What's been keeping you busy?" He turned those ocean-blue eyes on Abby.

Her gaze slipped from his eyes back to his full lips *Trying to forget our kiss.*

She ducked her head to keep from putting voice to her thoughts. "Nothing special." She shrugged. "Just the usual, grading papers, laundry."

Katie picked that moment to join in the conversation. "I've been trying to convince her that she needs to start dating."

Grant arched an eyebrow. "Really? And what did she say?" He spared a glance for Katie before returning his penetrating gaze on Abby.

"I told her I wasn't interested." Abby made the statement as much for her own benefit as everyone else's. Even if he was only a few years younger than her, getting involved with Jackson's brother-in-law was a recipe for disaster. She could just imagine the problems a badly ending relationship would cause for the two families.

The corner of his mouth quirked, revealing a dimple. "Why aren't you interested?"

She hadn't planned to tell Jackson and Katie her news tonight, but she was desperate to sidetrack this conversation. As well as help keep her mind off broad shoulders and blue eyes that kept shoving logic to the corner of her mind. She drew in a steading breath. "Because I'm going to be busy doing something else. I'll be beginning the second act of my life."

Abby looked towards Chris, who shot her thumbs up. After years of playing it safe, she was finally ready to step out of her comfort zone. Her new adventure was a risk she could handle. "I've been selected to participate in a teacher exchange program. At the end of this school year I'll be switching places with a teacher in England."

Grant's brows furrowed. "For how long?" His words were far more growling demand than polite inquiry.

"A, ye, a year." His reaction caught her off guard. "The woman's name is Laura Griffin. She and her two little girls will be living at my house while I stay in her flat."

Katie practically bounced in her seat. "A real trading places."

Abby checked in on the two men in her life. As she saw Jackson's smile matched Chris's, some of the tension eased from her. These three were the opinions that counted.

"True." Her thoughts wound to of the projects at home and in her classroom she wanted to do before she left. "I have about a million things to do between now and then." She turned to Jackson. "One of those will be to makeover your old bedroom for her girls."

Katherine leaned forward. "That's a lot of work. Are you sure you want to do that?"

Once Abby made up her mind about something, she was all in. No looking back. No second guessing her decision. "I am and want to get started right away."

Before the wedding, she'd offered Katie and Jackson the antique bedroom suite from his room at home. "Katie and Jackson are coming by Saturday with a moving van."

Grant raised his hand. "I'm free Saturday if you

need help moving."

Jackson jumped at the offer before she could decline. "That'd be great."

Grant stood. "I'll see you Saturday then." His gaze trained on Abby.

Her cheeks heated under his stare, and she mentally added another benefit to a year abroad. Not having to pretend she wasn't attracted to him. All she had to do was keep it together for one, maybe two more encounters with Mr. Sex-On-Legs. She could do that.

Surely.

Chapter Seven

As Grant pulled into Abby's driveway, his cell phone went off. "Hey, little sister."

His lips twitched, listening to her explanation for why she and Jackson were running late.

"Don't worry about it. I'll tell her y'all will be here in an hour."

Grant ended the call as he stepped out of the truck. "Thank you very much, baby sister."

Her tardiness was just the thing he needed to get some alone time with Katie's very sweet, very sexy mother-in-law.

He surveyed Abby's homestead, first checking out the brick patio, neatly trimmed shrubs and straw covered flowerbeds. Then he noted the tiny garage and ancient car sleeping inside. The car's green paint looked faded and he could see from ten yards away that the chrome bumper was rusted. A protective instinct twisted his gut at the thoughts of that POS leaving her stranded somewhere.

Grant filed that worry away for later action and moved towards her front door. As he brushed past azaleas, he tilted his head up for a weather check. The thin layer of clouds looked like they might break up. Maybe this would be one move where he didn't get soaked.

He mounted the stairs and took the seconds

between rapping on the door and her answering to enjoy the view from Abby's deep front porch. The Arts and Crafts bungalow was a little slice of middle class, right down to the white picket fence. Then she opened the door and all home and hearth thoughts flew right out of his head.

"Good morning." She smiled politely and stepped back so he could enter.

Once he could drag his eyes away from lips that begged to be tasted, he noticed she'd piled those honey-colored curls of hers into a loose twist and the only color on her face was natural. He eased passed her, wondering how much more she'd blush if he kissed her.

Stick to the plan.

Despite his imagination's insistence it needed a refresh, the best way to turn her "no" into an "oh my, Grant, please" was to a subtle approach, not an ambush. He just hadn't counted on seduction under a deadline. Less than five months. He didn't let himself think about what he'd do when she left for her new job. One problem at a time.

"Katie and Jackson are running late. They forgot to set their alarm." He used air-quotes to emphasize *forgot*.

Her lips twitched. "That's a new one. Last time it was a last-minute errand." She lost the battle to keep a straight face and chuckled. "Newlyweds."

He shrugged. "What can I say?"

"We were just finishing up breakfast." Abby pointed to the room beyond. "Would you like some?"

"Coffee would be good if you've got it."

What's this we business?

Grant stepped into her kitchen to find the non-boyfriend sitting so comfortably anyone would think he lived there. There were plates, coffee cups, and papers scattered over the tabletop. A real cozy scene Grant had walked into. How fan-fucking-tastic.

Chris stood to shake Grant's hand. "Good to see you again. How's the airplane business?"

"It's good." Grant ground his molars, trying like hell not to show his frustration at having his plans screwed.

"Chris and I were just going over the blueprints for the house in Charleston he's remodeling." Abby cleared the dishes off the table then set them in the sink. When she returned to the table, she spent the next several minutes telling him about the antebellum mansion and her friend's brilliant ideas.

The tension eased from Grant's shoulders listening to her dulcet voice, even if he was hearing Chris's plans for restoring the house's eight fireplaces. When the conversation lagged, he searched for a way to keep her going. Seeing her tidy black and white kitchen with its soapstone counters and checkerboard tile prompted a question. "When was your house built?"

"1928." She winked at her friend. "Although I haven't lived here that long." When Chris offered her a dramatic eye roll, she giggled like she was sixteen. "I know, bad joke," she admitted between chuckles.

Sweet baby Jesus, he loved a woman with a sense of humor, even when the smiles and giggles weren't trained on him. "I could listen to you laugh all day." The words left his mouth before he could catch them.

She met his gaze for the briefest second, her whiskey-colored eyes blazing into him. Then she bolted from her seat. "Would you like some breakfast? I made blueberry muffins."

What he wanted was to get her away from her human shield. "How about a tour? After hearing about your remodeling projects on our plane trip home, I'm interested in seeing your handiwork."

She folded her arms across her chest. "Umm... Sure. The bedrooms and baths are this way." She took a couple steps towards the dining room then looked over her shoulder at Chris. "Holler if you decide you want me to scramble you some eggs or if you want my input on the kitchen design."

Chris looked up from his coffee, his eyes narrowed.

"I'm good. Take your time."

Grant sent the guy mental thanks and followed her lead through her dining room and up a narrow hall. He'd have followed her over a cliff if he could watch the gentle swing of her hips as she moved.

She paused to let him see an example of a 1930s bathroom before moving up the hall. "Here's my room."

It looked like something from a movie set starring Bette Davis. She even had one of those mirrored dressing tables he'd seen in black and white movies. "Chris surprised me for my birthday a couple years ago and had a decorator do it over." She ran her hand over the pale blue comforter. "It's a little fancy for me. I always feel like I should be wearing satin instead of flannel in here."

He spared a couple brains cells to recognize she was once again drawing Chris into the room, even if he wasn't physically there. Mostly his mind was occupied with conjuring up a hi-def picture of her dressed in a silky nightgown, her hair all loose around her shoulders. He most definitely could see her in this room. Grant could also imagine himself in here with her too. "I think it suits you." He eased behind her. His slow and subtle resolve was weakening. All he'd have to do is lean in and taste her skin.

She spun on her heals. "Let me show you the furniture I'm giving Katie and Jackson."

More antique furniture. Only this wasn't just old, it was heavy, like it had been made from whole tree trunks.

"It's very nice of you to give it to Katie and Jackson."

"It was the suite my parents bought as newlyweds, so it seemed fitting." She maintained a safe three-foot buffer between them.

He kept to the safe topic of home improvement and didn't crowd her like his body was screaming to. "What are you going to do in here?"

"I found a pair of twin beds and a dresser at a secondhand shop for next to nothing. Chris and I are going to refinish them." She gestured towards the room's wide window. "Then I'm going to make a window seat so the exchange program teacher's girls can curl up and read."

"That should keep you busy."

She started pulling the drawers out of the dresser and stacking them on the bed. "That's the goal. I've been restless lately."

Restless?

Hell, caged tigers were calmer. From the moment he'd stepped in her house, she hadn't lit in one spot for more than a few seconds. Grant arched an eyebrow.

"Winter blues?" He cued into her moving target tactics meant she was feeling the heat on her side as well.

Abby's eyes lingered over him then darted away. "Something like that." She moved to a nightstand and snatched it up like it weighed nothing. "What you say we get started loading this furniture."

She *so* wasn't going to carry the darn thing all the way to his truck. Not while he had arms and legs. He cut off her path and eased his arms around the piece of furniture. They brushed across hers as she relinquished the nightstand. "I've got this."

"Chris, we need a little more muscle in here."

Grant lumbered through the house, making it to his truck just as the skies opened. Between wrestling the tarp and the rain blinding him, the next several trips were markedly more arduous than if Mother Nature had cooperated. Kinda made him think of another lady who wasn't making things easy.

With the last piece of furniture loaded and covered, Grant followed her back into the kitchen. He looked at the blueprints still scattered across her kitchen table. "Are you and Chris coming to my mom's party?"

She handed him a towel, looked up at him from a fringe of dark lashes. "It'll just be me."

"I thought you two were joined at the hip."

"I can see why you might think that. But he has a date."

Maybe fate wasn't working against him after all. He bit the inside of his mouth to keep from smiling. "Good for him, and since after May you'll miss a whole year's worth of Mom's parties, you can't miss any of them between now and then."

Chapter Eight

Abby eased her car onto Katherine's drive, but only after passing muster at the main gate of Hillgrove subdivision, North Atlanta's premier gated community. Aided by flood lamps that shone into the bare limbs of dozens of oak trees, she wound her car down the quarter mile path that separated the mansion from the street. "I've never met anybody who loved to entertain more than this woman." She noted strands of twinkling lights wrapped around the mansion's Doric columns.

Abby killed the engine but didn't reach for the door handle. Knowing Katherine's many soirées were never casual affairs, Abby first needed to gird her loins. She flipped down the vanity mirror, checking her lipstick, and then brushed a hand over the hair she'd spent an hour straightening before finally stepping from her car.

After *Westminster Bells* announced her arrival, a maid ushered her inside. Abby scanned the crowd milling around Katherine's great room. Teetering between anticipation and dread, she wondered not *if* but *when* she'd see Grant. She just hoped she'd be able to control her ever increasing reaction to his presence.

"Abby." Katherine's southern drawl echoed in the cavernous foyer. "Don't you look just darling in that color. I'm so glad you came."

Turning her attention to her hostess, Abby arranged her lips into a smile. "Thank you for inviting me." Then she looked at Katherine's chic ensemble, thankful her intuition warned the dress code for this party would be slightly more upscale than the parties she typically attended. Instead of jeans and sweatshirt, Abby wore a nice pair of black trousers and the plum-colored cashmere sweater Chris had given her for Christmas.

"Come in and let me get you a drink." Katherine took Abby by the elbow.

Finally, after half an hour of making small talk with strangers, Abby caught a glimpse of a familiar face as Katie breezed into the great room. She latched onto her daughter-in-law. "How was your week?"

"Crazy." She rolled her eyes. "I want to ask you about some differentiation strategies when we can get a moment to talk. First, I want you to meet someone."

Following Katie into a kitchen the size of her house, Abby's gaze immediately zeroed in on the large, male at the far end of the room. Dressed in faded jeans and work boots, Grant made the rest of the party's male guests seem about as masculine as the lacy curtains hanging in her kitchen.

He didn't notice her as she drew closer, which was just as well since there was no way in heck she could hide her reaction to seeing him. Abby's cheeks heated as he studied the laptop before him, knowing what it was like to be the focus of that intensity.

After taking him in and finding nothing wanting, her attention turned to the slender blonde across from him. Wearing an ivory suit with her hair pulled back in a tidy bun, the woman seemed to be working with Grant on some type of project. Abby tried to place the woman, ticking through the dozens she'd met at Katie's numerous bridal showers but came up blank.

Katie gave Abby a gentle push towards the couple. "Look who's here."

The woman rose gracefully from the table and enfolded Katie in a hug. "How's married life?"

"Heather, it's wonderful. You should try it again."

"Fat chance."

Katie drew Abby closer. "This is my mother-in-law, Abby."

Heather's eyes widened. "Nice to meet you." She extended a hand. "I've heard your name quite a lot lately."

It was Abby's turn for a wide-eyed reaction, but Katie quickly provided the context under which she'd been the topic of conversation. "Since you teach children with special needs, I thought you wouldn't mind letting Grant and Heather pick your brain."

Heather patted Abby on the arm, the woman's flawless features forming a kind smile. "But we don't want to keep you from the party if you'd rather."

Feeling immediately at ease with the woman, Abby quickly responded, "Believe me. I don't think I'm missing anything."

"Then sit." Grant pulled out a chair for her. "I was afraid you wouldn't come tonight. You didn't sound too excited when we talked the other day."

She hadn't been until now. With him sitting next to her, she was suddenly glad she'd forgone her other options. "I try to keep my promises."

Grant's eyes deepened in color and a moment passed where he seemed to be conveying a message. "An admirable quality."

Katie patted Abby on the shoulder. "My work here is done. I better get back to the party."

Abby shifted in her seat. "What can I do to help?"

Grant handed her a folded piece of paper. A collage of photos featuring families in different home and recreational settings filled the brochure. "Heather and I started the Help and Hope Foundation after our daughter Grace was diagnosed with autism." He shot a glance towards Heather. "Our goal is to help other families facing the same struggles as us."

Abby's gaze bounced between Heather and Grant, the proverbial light bulb going off. Katie told her some of this family's history, about the divorce and Grace's diagnosis. The apparent closeness of the former spouses caught her off guard. The comfortable way they finished each other's sentences reminded her of Chris and herself.

Turning her thoughts from the pair, she read the brochure. She'd heard of the foundation from some of her students' parents without realizing she knew one of the founders. As she read the information, she learned Help and Hope provided support groups and respite care for parents in addition to providing funds for therapies insurance didn't cover.

Except at the wedding when his devotion to Katie had been evident, all Grant showed the world was a rich, charming man out for a good time. This new facet touched her soul. "That's truly remarkable."

Heather beamed. "I'm glad you think so. We like to have members from the community sit on the board of directors, and our education liaison resigned last week." She arched an elegant eyebrow. "Would you consider taking a position?"

"I'd love to…" Her gaze darted to Grant and her excitement ebbed just as quickly as it peaked. She used the excuse easiest to explain. “I can’t. I’m leaving the country at the end of May. I’ll be gone an entire year so I cannot commit to anything.”

Heather’s smile faltered. “That’s too bad.” A chime from her phone announced a text and she picked up the device to read the incoming message.

While the woman’s attention was diverted, Abby eyed Grant. His cobalt-blue eyes did things to her she was better off not thinking about.

“That’s my Mother.” Heather stood and gathered her coat and purse. “Grace is having a hard time settling down for the night. I better go.”

Grant placed a palm on his ex-wife’s arm. “I can handle it if you’d like.”

She waved off his offer. “You stay. See if you can sweet talk Abby into changing her mind.”

“Tell your mom I said thanks for looking after our girl.”

As Heather left through the kitchen’s back door, Abby braced for the onslaught of charm.

He shook his head as if he’d read her mind. “No spiel. But would you at least think about taking the position?”

Her gaze trailed across a pair of broad shoulders and up to his strong jaw. His blue eyes melted her resolve to do the sensible thing. “Okay, I’ll think about it.”

“Good.” The corners of his generous mouth turned up.

His smile made her want to agree to things other than charity work. Several seconds passed before she realized she was staring.

I need a diversion if I’m going to make it out of this

kitchen without making a fool of myself.

"Do you have a picture of Grace?"

"Of course." He pulled his phone from his hip pocket, opened the photo app and passed it to her.

Abby flipped through several pictures of the little girl playing outside, surrounded by toy dogs, and sleeping. "My goodness, she's beautiful."

"She definitely got her mother's looks."

Abby expanded a snap of Grace sitting on a rocking horse. "I see you in there too. She's got your lips and chin."

He laughed. "Thankfully, she didn't get my nose."

She shook her head. There wasn't one thing about his looks that wasn't practically perfect. "You have a nice nose. It suits your face."

He took the phone, stowing it in his pocket. His face grew serious as he turned his attention to her. "She's my reason for getting up in the morning."

Such tenderness.

"She's a lucky little girl."

"I'm the lucky one, and while I'm not ready to say her autism is a blessing, it has made me a better man. It really got me to see just paying the bills isn't what makes a good father. Being there for your kid is."

His honesty did more to disarm her than all his dimpled smiles. "What if I pitched in on the Board until I leave? That should give you time to get someone who can serve long-term."

His brow furrowed. "You sure? As much as I want you to do this, I don't want you to feel pressured."

"Yeah, I'm sure." She reached for his hand. The strength she felt as he returned her squeeze did something warm and wonderful to her insides. She upturned his hand in hers slowly stroking his calloused palm.

He tugged it away. "Sorry, my hands are a mess."

She stopped him before he could tuck them in his lap. Pulling them both towards her, she wove her fingers with his. "No, there's something very honest about them."

Grant's eyes were heavy on her and he unwound one of his hands to trail lightly up her arm. When he cupped her cheek, she leaned into his touch, finding something alluring about a hard man with a soft spot for his family. Their lips touched for an instant before footsteps drove them apart.

Jackson trotted into the room, making a beeline for the refrigerator. Then spying her, he detoured. "What are you doing in here?"

Abby clenched her eyes to erase the vision of what he might have seen had his entry been quieter.

He tugged on her arm. "Come say hello to everyone downstairs."

She glanced up at Grant, for the first time reluctant to escape his presence. "I probably should go."

With a grin, Grant clasped Jackson's shoulder. "I'll bring her down in a few minutes. First, I want to take your mom on the fifty-cent tour." Not giving Jackson a chance to argue, Grant motion to her. "Come on. I'll make sure we're in the game room in time to watch the halftime show."

The instant Jackson disappeared, Grant pulled Abby into the tiny space off from the dining room.

"What are you doing?" She looked around at his mother's hoard of silver and china. "This is the butler's pantry."

"The tour has to start somewhere." His arm snaked around Abby's waist, craving another taste of her lips.

She placed a palm on his chest. "This is a bad idea."

Her lips might be saying one thing, but the vein thrumming in her neck told him otherwise. Grant tilted her chin and growled. "Seems like a particularly good idea to me. Besides, you want me too."

She screwed her eyes closed and nodded. "Wanting's not the problem."

"Then tell me why."

"Because…"

She'd done something to her hair to make it straight and under the room's light the golden color shimmered. He fingered a lock, needing to see if it felt as silky as it looked.

"I can't think when you're doing that." She turned away from him.

He had to get her out of her head if they were ever going to get any farther than this torturous waltz they were doing. "That's the point. You think way too much. What if, what if, what if." He could practically hear the thoughts churning through her mind.

Her whisky-colored eyes had turned a deep brown. "Don't you worry that you'd regret this?"

"Never." No need to even ponder her question. "I only regret the things I haven't done." That list was plenty long enough. He never regretted the chances he'd taken, even when they didn't turn out the way he wanted. He brushed a thumb across her cheek. "Would you like me to tell you some of the things I regret not doing?"

She ducked her chin. "If you like."

"I regret not doing this by the pool." He cupped the back of her head and fused their mouths in a punishing kiss. The moan that escaped her only fueled his need. He parted her lips and slipped his tongue into her mouth. Grant tangled his tongue with hers, tasting a minty sweetness that did little to extinguish the building heat. Seeing her eyelids flutter close with pleasure, he grew bolder and crushed her body to his. "I regret letting you walk away from me in the hanger."

Grant wanted to roar with masculine satisfaction as she melted into him. He placed a light kiss on the apple of her cheek. "I should have done this when you were here last week."

"Oh yeah." She smiled up at him. "How would you have accomplished that? There were four other people in the room."

He kissed the other cheek. "What's a friendly kiss between in-laws?"

She shook her head. "You're incorrigible." Her laugh made the reprimand sound like the best compliment he'd ever received.

"Without a doubt." He brushed back her tresses, baring the slender column of ivory skin. "That neck of yours tempts me." He nipped her just behind the ear before soothing the tender flesh with his tongue. "This is what I should have done when you were showing me your house."

They were both panting before he stopped. "No more regrets." Never. No matter how things turned out with her.

Her body tensed as her breaths became more regular. "I should go. Jackson will be looking for me soon."

He pulled away. "I'll make a brazen woman out of you yet." In truth, she'd already given him far more than he could have hoped.

The corners of her mouth turned up. "I doubt that. Will you settle for one that's easily persuaded by a handsome face? I'd still like to volunteer with Help and Hope if you like."

"I haven't run you off."

She ducked her chin. "I seem to do that a lot around you."

"The lady who was heading up the family day picnic next month left all her information about corporate sponsors and things she'd purchased on a flash drive. I'll come by Wednesday after work and drop if off."

"Okay. She backed out of the small room. "Are you coming?"

"You go ahead." Yeah, he was going to have to hang out with the candlesticks and punch bowls for a few minutes while he regained control of himself. He watched her leave, hoping this wasn't the only time he'd ever get to hold her.

Chapter Nine

Abby braced the cell phone between her shoulder and ear, keeping her hands free so she could talk and dust at the same time. With Chris working in Charleston during the week, she was seriously behind on her "friend time." She couldn't remember the last time they'd gone five days without speaking.

"How was Katherine's party?"

She hadn't come anywhere near a television during her time at Katherine's. After Abby left the pantry, she'd been too flustered to pretend normalcy, so she'd quickly said her goodbyes and left. Her mind played over the reason she'd been too flustered to stay. Good heavens the way Grant's hands felt on her body.

"Abby, are you there?"

And those soft as suede lips. "What?"

"I asked about the Queen of Atlanta's party. You did go, didn't you?"

She had to clear her throat before she could answer. "It was fine." It was a good thing they were having this conversation over the phone, otherwise she'd never be able to fool him. She touched her cheeks, feeling their heat.

Pulling her thoughts to other matters, she remembered he'd had his own plans that night. "How was your date?"

He made a chuffing noise, the one he always paired

with a dramatic eye roll. "Let's just say if the guy was a dot-com executive, then I'm a straight guy. I hate people who feel they must lie on their profiles. Like a high-powered job negates being an ass."

"I'm sorry. It's his loss. I wish you were here so we could drown your sorrows in some ice cream."

He let out a small laugh, one that let her know just how disappointed he was with his date. "Tell me, what are you getting up to without me to keep you out of trouble?

"Nothing much." Saying something about grading papers or reading tempted her. She'd never lied to her best friend, and she wasn't going to start now. She just needed to make it sound like no big deal. "Katie's brother is coming over in a few minutes."

Several seconds ticked by. "Is it a date?"

"No." Her voice rose several octaves. It wasn't. A date involved some type of social activity. "I've agreed to help him with his autism charity, and he's bringing me some computer files he wants me to look over."

"That's too bad." He chuckled. "Grant is a fine specimen of the male gender."

Wasn't that the God's honest truth.

"Why are all the good ones either taken or straight?"

Abby fumbled the phone, she laughed so hard. "You're a mess."

The doorbell dried up her mirth. Her eyes darted around her living room as her free hand fluttered over her hair. "Hey, that's the door." She walked towards the sound of the bell that had rung again. "I better go."

"Don't do anything I wouldn't do."

"Jeez, that leaves what, skydiving and busty

blonds?"

The last part of her sentence hung in the air as she opened the door. She didn't know who was more surprised: Abby or her sister, Sarah, who was standing bug-eyed where her tall, dark and handsome should have been. Abby coughed to cover the laugh that threatened to bubble up.

"What? Who's there? Is Grant dressed in a Superman costume?"

They'd never been the type of sisters who just dropped by each other's place. Why now, of all times? "It's Sarah." Abby forced lightness into her response. No sense starting off on the wrong foot with her sister's visit.

"Don't let her get under your skin."

"Okay, I'll tell her you said hi." She pushed the End button on the phone.

Sarah stepped through the doorway. "I was in the area, and I thought I'd pop by and pick up those photos you promised."

After leaving Katie and Jackson's wedding on less than cordial terms, Abby wanted to smooth things over with the only blood relative she had other than Jackson. She'd made a small album of wedding photos to give as an olive branch. "It's right over here." She pointed to a bookcase behind her.

Her sister surveyed the room with a narrow gaze. "Are you expecting company?" Sarah pointed to the chips and salsa on the coffee table.

"Grant Davis is coming over in a while." Abby crossed her fingers behind her back and prayed her sister would cut her impromptu visit short.

Sarah cocked an eyebrow. "Isn't he married?"

The implication hurt. "He's divorced." If Abby did a thousand things right, it would never erase her one mistake in her sister's eyes. "Besides, it's not like that. I'm helping him and Heather with their charity."

Sarah narrowed her eyes as if she were calling up some detail from her memory banks. "They still live together, don't they?"

Classic Sarah. She loved gathering tidbits of information the way a squirrel did acorns. The better to judge everyone with.

Abby clenched her jaw to keep the storm of words inside her mouth. What business was it of Sarah's how other people lived their lives?

Sarah prattled on, keeping up her one-sided conversation. "Makes you wonder if the two of them can stand to live under the same roof why they didn't just stay married."

A chill washed over Abby. She saw last Sunday how well the two got on. Like friends. What if there was more than co-parenting going on?

Sarah continued to prattle on, unaware of how her words effected Abby. "Who knows, maybe they'll remarry. I always think it's best if children are raised in a two-parent home."

Abby seethed from her sister's latest jab. She could name quite a few children who turned out fine with one parent.

Jackson.

And a few who'd been raised with both parents who seemed to delight in making each other miserable. She'd had all the family values lecture she could stand. Abby grabbed the album off the shelf and thrust it towards her sister. "I hope you'll enjoy the pictures."

Her words came out as a growl. So much for the olive branch.

Sarah blinked, seemingly confused by Abby's forcefulness. Her sister always acted surprised when others didn't share her point of view or baulked at being schooled on morality. Her mouth opened as if she were about to launch into another round of "what's wrong with the world."

Abby's phone cut off the impending lecture. Grant's number showed up on the phone's screen. She took a breath and prayed for calm. "Hello, there."

His sultry voice reached out to her. "Hi, beautiful."

She held up a finger to her sister and stepped out of earshot. "What's up?"

"Something's come up here at home." Though his voice became muffled, probably from him covering the receiver with his palm, she could still hear him say, "Hold on sweetheart. I'll be right there." Then his voice became clear again. "I'll call you, and we can reschedule."

Images of the cozy scene playing in the background flooded her mind. "Okay, that's fine." She ended the call then schooled her features into a placid mask before turning back to her sister.

Sarah quirked an eyebrow.

"Grant had to cancel." Not that she owed her sister an explanation, it just made sense to downplay things with Sarah.

Her lips formed a thin line. "I think that's probably for the best."

Perhaps it was.

"He'll email me the files later."

Sarah tucked the photo album into her purse. "I

should be going. I don't want to be late for choir practice."

With her sister on her way, Abby fell against the closed door. She pressed her head between open palms in a vain attempt to stop the words that played inside her head on a continuous loop. When Abby discovered the last guy she was dating was still married, she swore the next man who claimed to be divorced had to present his legal papers before she'd go out with him. Maybe that wasn't enough to ensure she didn't repeat the same mistake. Yeah, email, DIY projects, and distance sounded like a better insurance policy.

****

There was absolutely nothing fun about watching a little girl be miserable, especially one who couldn't easily convey her needs. First, Grace had run a low-grade temperature then came the stomach issues. Next, Heather came down with the virus and he became Daddy-on-duty.

"Your old man's trying to make it better." Grant patted her leg as she lay curled up on the sofa. "Do you want one of your buddies to keep you company?" He danced one of her stuffed animals across the coffee table before tucking it in next to her. "It's so bad to have a fever." He pressed a kiss to her forehead, feeling the heat from her one-hundred-degree fever. "Bless your heart, baby."

On top of the typical discomfort of the flu, there was the communication issues that came with autism. She'd been in speech therapy since her diagnosis and made gains in expressive language. However, he still needed to use his dad's intuition to gauge just how bad she felt. Finally, after another dose of medicine and a popsicle, she dosed off.

Grant should have used the time to catch up on work emails, instead he watched Grace sleep. And thought about Abby. Hopefully, everyone would be well enough that the next Board meeting of Help and Hope could take place next week. Abby was scheduled to attend and he'd get an opportunity to spend time with her then. For the time being he'd focus on helping his daughter get well.

****

Friday's were Abby's day to stay late at school to catch up on paperwork. With Jackson married and living his own life, Chris out of town, and no social life outside of family, there was nothing to rush home to.

Lauren Mason, Abby's co-teacher, entered their classroom with an armload of copies for next week's assignments. "This week seems like it's been a month long."

Abby kept her eyes on the six-inch stack of special education documents due on Monday. "No kidding. The time between now and Spring Break always feels the longest."

This school year was the first she and Miss Mason had worked as a team. She enjoyed the young woman's energy, but today she'd looked like she'd keel over. Between kids getting sick in the classroom, an unannounced fire drill, and a student who had behavior issues having a meltdown, they were both due a break.

Lauren pulled out a container of sanitizing wipes from her desk drawer and began the daily ritual of wiping down the classroom. "Hopefully, we're reaching the end of flu season. How many kids were out this week?"

Abby counted in her head. "Eight." She drew a circle in the air, indicating the perimeter of the classroom. "Have you noticed the Pattern? It looks like it's creeping across the classroom."

Lauren lifted her free hand to cover her eyes. "And I'm directly in its path."

The first year Abby had been in the classroom, she'd caught every bug that went through the room. Twenty years later, her immune system had grown tougher than a rhino's hide. "Better go home and rest up. Drink plenty of fluids and dose-up on Vitamin C."

The other teacher turned from the stack of chairs she'd been wiping down, a grin making her face shine. "Actually, some of us were meeting at Wild Bob's for adult recess." She used air quotes when she used teacher speak for a party where they got to let their hair down.

Abby had joined a few of those over the years. "Sounds fun. Enjoy. You've earned it."

Having finished her war on germs, Lauren joined Abby at the front of the room where both of their desks were located. "Do you and Chris have plans for tonight?"

Abby had been teased over the years about her relationship with her bestie being like an old married couple. However, he was finally making good on his plans to find a guy to share his life with. "Not this weekend. He had a date." At least one of them might have a shot at happily ever after.

"Come along, then. It'll be fun."

"Can't. I've got somewhere to be in a couple hours." The prospect of seeing Grant had her stomach fluttering, but it had also gotten her through a week filled with fractions, student meltdowns, and paperwork. He was like the promise of chocolate cake at the end of a week of dieting. "Perhaps another time."

"You got a date?"

Abby's blush gave her away. "Noooo."

"You do, don't you."

She shrugged and repeated the mantra she'd told herself all week. "It's a meeting. There'll be at least five other people there."

Lauren planted her hip on Abby's desk. "Then what's the big deal? I've never seen your cheeks turn this pink. Not even when one of the Atlanta Braves came for spirit day."

What exactly was the big deal?

Every time she and Grant were in the same room, his gaze tracked her every move. He also never missed an opportunity to touch her, but other than that one kiss nothing romantic was happening. They weren't even friends. "I'm going to be helping a group of parents with a charity they'd started. I've been asked to sit on the Board. Until I leave for my year abroad."

"Right. What's the guy's name?"

"I never said it was a guy."

Lauren pointed a finger in Abby's direction. "You didn't have to. Since when do you dress up on a jeans day?"

So what if she'd worn her boots with the spikey heels and spent a few extra minutes with her hair and makeup. It never hurt to look nice. "Don't let me keep you from your recess."

Lauren popped off the desk. "Shoot. I don't want to be late." She grabbed her purse and coat. At the doorway she paused. "I expect a full report on your *meeting* on Monday."

Abby patted her cheeks, still feeling the heat from her blush. With enough self-control there'd be nothing to tell her young coworker.

Problem was she couldn't decide how she wanted the evening to go.

****

Grant drummed a pen against the mahogany dining table. Even the most focused of men would have a hard time following the drone of information that could have been an email. Add in the woman who filled most of his thoughts and the meeting might as well been in French for all he retained of the board members' updates.

Heather stood. "Before we adjourn, I'd like to take this chance to thank Abby Roberts for taking over from Miss Owen. She's really jumped in with both feet with her suggestions for our Family Day picnic."

As Grant predicted she would, the recipient of the praise ducked her head, smiling modestly. "I'm very glad to help."

Heather continued, "If no one else has anything further, I move we adjourn the meeting."

A chorus of "seconds" and "ayes" erupted from the people gathered around the dining room table in the house he'd bought for Grace.

Predicting Abby would make a speedy get away, he had a plan already in place. Before she could gather her purse and coat, he circled the table. "I need to ask you a couple quick questions before you leave." He positioned himself between her and the foyer.

Her eyes darkened for a split second before she hid her emotions behind a plastic smile. She glanced over her shoulder at the other board members who were following Heather into the foyer. “I might have someone blocked in the driveway.”

“Why didn’t you return my calls.” Between searching for food Grace would eat and watching episodes of her favorite dog videos, he’d sent Abby several texts. And emails. And voice messages.

“I emailed you the list of possible corporate sponsors and the information about the stables offering hippotherapy.”

“I got them, thank you.” The sight of her golden hair, the curling ends touching the tops of her breasts had taunted him from across the table. He took one of the spirals between two fingers. “I realized earlier today that I didn’t do a very good job of explaining what was going on with Heather and Grace.

Since making that first phone call, he’d had a knot in his gut that had nothing to do with the sickness that had invaded his house. As the week progressed and Abby hadn’t returned his calls, he realized she wasn’t going to willingly listen to an explanation. Even if she deserved one. Other than camping out in the school’s parking lot—which sounded a lot like stalking—he’d run out of options. The monthly board meeting of Help and Hope was the only chance he’d get to see Abby until his mother’s next party.

“That’s not necessary.”

“Heather and Grace came down with the flu and that’s why I had to cancel.” As much as he hated to cancel on Abby, some things were unavoidable.

Again with the placid smile. He’d have much rather endured some “hell hath no fury” than her “I am an island” imitation.

“Naturally, and you had to take care of both of

them."

"I'm the last person Heather wants for that, but I did need to look after Grace."

"Of course. Well, thank you for letting me know. I hope your family stays well."

Grant held up his hands, pleading. "It's not like that." He could easily see how someone would jump to the wrong conclusion. "After the divorce we tried having Grace spend half the week with each of us, but that was really rough on her. With her autism, she needs the consistency of living in one place. Since neither of us wanted to give up our time with her, I bought this house."

"Y'all really do all live here together?" She eyed the main living area.

Grant shook his head. "Heather has a condo in the city, and I stay in the gatehouse here on the property, so we don't exactly get cozy over the breakfast table, but after a lot of compromise, some ground rules, and more than a few arguments, we've finally found a system that works for everyone."

Abby's brow furrowed. "I don't understand. You and Heather seem to get along so well."

"We try to be on our best behavior." A terse conversation the two of them had last week about an overflowing trash can reminded him just how fragile their working relationship was. "As long as we keep things to the Help and Hope foundation and Grace, we manage."

"It sounds like an ingenious plan." She touched his arm, her stiff smile replaced with a warm, gentle look. "Another of the things you do very well."

He seized the thaw in the icy wall she'd surrounded

herself with, taking her by the hand and pulling her into the library where they could talk in private. "I've put up with a lot of crap from people over my living arrangements with Heather, but all I've ever wanted to do is to look after my family and be a good dad to Grace."

This was the man that kept drawing Abby back, entangling her more fully each time she caught a glimpse. "You're one of the best men I've ever known." Then she touched her lips to his cheek. The feel of his whiskers against her lips as she feathered kisses across his jaw ignite a fire in her belly and changed her admiration into lust. Their lips met then moved slowly, deepening with each touch. Responding to his heated touch she sank deeper into him.

He groaned against her mouth. "That feels so good."

Abby jerked away from his embrace.

Have I lost my mind?

She touched her fingers to her lips. "I'm sorry, I shouldn't have done that."

He captured her hands but stopped short of pulling her back. "I'm not." His hand trailed up her arm to cup her cheek. "In fact, I'd like to do more than that."

She shook her head. "I'm not trying to get you to chase me, or some silliness like that."

He stared at her from hooded eyes, seeing through her better than an x-ray. "I never thought you were. You're just a little on the careful side."

Her answer held a plea for understanding as well as an explanation. "I am, for a reason. Listen, I'm terrible with relationships."

He barked out a laugh that held a cold edge.

"You're saying it's you, not me."

Her mouth crooked up. "No, it's definitely me." Abby's heartbeat ticked off the seconds as she waited for him to respond.

The icy blue of his eyes had softened to the color of worn denim. "I'm not asking for all of you." His hand brushed over her hair as he spoke. "If you can only give a small piece of yourself, I'll take it. Just so long as you'll let me have something of you."

Her resolve hung by the finest of threads. "You make saying 'no' very hard."

His hands were suddenly pulling her back. "Then don't."

Abby attacked his mouth, dying to recapture the hungry feel of his kisses. She leaned in, loving the way the hard plane of his chest felt against her breast.

After a moment that didn't last nearly long enough, he pulled back enough to survey her cautiously. "Is that a yes to something?"

She smoothed her hand along the sharp edge of his jaw. "It's something, but God if I could tell you what it is."

As Grant began kissing her again, Abby's breath came in pants.

He brushed back a lock of her spiraling hair. "I'm willing to let this be on your terms."

"How do you always know the right thing to say?" She caressed the angle of his jaw.

His smile broadened, giving her a glimpse of his dimple. "Give me a minute, and I'll probably say something stupid to screw things up."

She laughed. "Then let's don't talk for a while."

Once all the board members had cleared the foyer,

he led her out of the house. The two of them stumbled in the dark over to the cottage door. "I can't believe I'm asking this, but are you sure?"

Her pulse thrummed in her ears knowing one more step and there'd be no going back. "Is this how it feels to jump out of a perfectly good airplane?"

"Pretty much." Then he led her inside.

Chapter Ten

Abby barely noticed the open space and clean, modern lines of his cottage, too focused on Grant's hands as he unbuttoned her blouse. He pulled hungrily, sending a couple buttons flying. When he'd loosened the last button, his movements slowed. Brushing the blouse from her shoulders, his fingers traced the lace cups of her bra before cupping her breasts. "You're beautiful."

She felt beautiful. How could she not the way he worshiped her? "Make love to me, Grant, please."

With a wicked grin and a flash of dimple, he began backing them down a hallway. "I have every intention to, beautiful." When they reached his bedroom, he scooped her onto the biggest bed she'd ever seen. Nothing about this man seemed moderate or ordinary, especially not the way his attention focused on the job at hand.

As intense as the feel of his mouth was, she wanted, no she *needed* more of him. Fisting his sweater, she pulled him closer.

Grant pulled away, kissing her hands as he extracted himself from her grasp. "Patience. We've waited too long to rush this." He ripped his sweater over his head. "Besides, this is too rough to be next to your tender skin."

Abby trembled as the heat from his hand sent

tendrils of desire licking through her body.

"You're shaking. Here let me cover you."

He did. With his body. Then he fused their lips in a kiss. "You were so worth the wait. I want to make love with you until we both forget everything that's come before."

After the lovemaking, he collapsed beside her and they lay breathless on top of the covers. "I'd give everything I own to spend the rest of my life doing that with you," he murmured before closing his eyes.

No one had ever laid themselves so bare to her the way he did. She squeezed her eyes to block the image of the two of them fulfilling Grant's wish. As she descended from her euphoria she reminded herself, one perfect hour did not a future make.

****

Lying on his belly, Grant metered his breathing, pretending to doze as he lay inches from Abby's bare body. The urge to cocoon her had him nearly as amped-up as before they'd made love. But crowding her, even as she slept, was probably the last thing she wanted given he'd already had an attack of way-over-sharing.

So much for your promise to give her space.

He reined in the urge to run his palm over the flat plane of her stomach by planning an extended, slow motion round two.

When the bed dipped as she eased off it, he rolled on his side in time to catch a spectacular view of her bare back. "Hey." He reached for her, brushing his fingers across the back of her hand. "Where are you going?"

Abby looked over her shoulder as she worked her black lace panties up her long legs. "I need to get home."

His pulse, which thanks to the vivid imagery his brain had been cooking up, hadn't returned to normal range. Watching her leave his bed had it kicking into aerobic levels. She couldn't be going so soon.

Grant levered upright, looking for signs of regret. "Are you okay?"

She scooted back on the bed and folded her legs underneath her. Watching her sitting naked to the waist and inches from him wasn't helping him give her space. He singled out a spiraling tendril of her hair to wrap around his finger. "Having regrets?"

Her teeth bit into her bottom lip. Then after a long moment she shook her head. "Are you?"

He gave up the pretense of giving her space, pulling her onto his lap. After kissing her lightly, he feathered more across her cheek. "Goodness, no. How could I?"

She let him hold her for a few precious moments before she eased herself back to peek up at him. "I learned something about you just now."

He didn't think his desire for her would come as a surprise given the growing erection beneath her or the fact that even on his very-best-good day subtlety wasn't his strong suit. "You did?"

Her smile spread from her lips upward until her whiskey-colored eyes sparked. "You make love like you live."

He barked out a laugh. "Are you saying I'm an impulsive lover or a pushy one?"

"No, a wide open and full tilt one."

He clamped his lips together to keep from asking if that was a good thing.

Give her space.

But when she slid from his arms and began fumbling on the floor for her pants, he couldn't let her go. "I really did want to ask you a couple questions earlier."

"It wasn't just a ploy to get me down here?" Mischief danced in her eyes.

"No, just the happy result."

"I really do need to go." Her eyes pleaded as she headed for the other room.

Grabbing his own clothes, he reached the living room in time to see her breasts swaying like a pair of erotic pendulums as she leaned over to snag her hastily discarded clothes off the floor. Then he watched mesmerized while she eased the straps over her shoulders and fastened the lace cups of her bra. Not nearly as much fun as seeing the process in reverse but sexy as hell to see her fingers move across her perfectly smooth skin.

Abby buttoned up "Come shopping with me tomorrow. We can talk then."

"Sure."

She reached for her coat but he got to it first and held it open for her to shrug into.

"I'd like for us to spend more time together without other people around."

"Heck, I'll hold your purse and wait outside the dressing room if you want."

Abby shook her head. "You really do know how to say just the right thing."

"I'll remind you of that the next time I put my size thirteens in my mouth."

"It's a deal." A smile played at her lips. "You're in

luck. It's not that type of shopping. I have to go to the hardware store, the party supply place, and a bedding store. It's all things either for the Help and Hope's family day or the bedroom I'm redoing for the two little Griffin girls."

A jolt of urgency fired off in his brain at the reminder she'd be leaving in three months. But, since she was getting ready to walk out his door any second now, he shoved down-the-road worries to the side in favor of the one staring him in the face.

When she took another step towards the door, he lunged for her, taking her by the shoulders. Taking advantage of the chance to hold her a little longer, he began fastening the buttons of her coat. Then because she was letting him, he eased her hair from under the collar of her coat, fanning it over her shoulders. "I'll pick you up around noon?"

She stood on her toes to press a light kiss against his lips. "No. I'll meet you at the North Atlanta Avenues."

Chapter Eleven

"See if I buy you new floor mats." Abby chuckled as she slammed the car door. After twenty minutes, several promises, and threats to get the jumper cables after her car, she admitted defeat. Harvey the car was DOA and Grant was going to get his way. She palmed her phone on her way back inside. It rang once.

"Not cancelling on me, are you?"

"No." She shook her head at what appeared to be his method of answering a call—no greeting, straight to the point. "My car died."

"That's too bad." His mock sympathy had her laughing. He had a way of doing that to her, helping her see the fun side of situations. "I guess I get to chauffeur you around after all."

Abby sat down at her desk in the corner of her living room and powered up her laptop. "Somehow I knew that would please you."

"Only because it gives me another chance to get you into a confined space where you can't escape."

The purr in his voice shot her thoughts to the butler's pantry, the point when she realized not only could she no longer resist him, but she didn't want to. A spark of heat bloomed in her at the deep rumble of his voice.

"I'll see you in a few minutes then."

Fanning herself with a stack of papers, Abby

opened her email's inbox. After cleaning out the notices from the neighborhood watch and the ads the spam filter didn't catch, she opened one from the woman with whom she'd be trading places.

The majority of Laura Griffin's cheery letter contained a dozen questions about life in Atlanta, but her closing included the number eighty-three: the number of days until they met in Washington D.C. for orientation. Already amped up from her conversation with Grant, Abby now practically vibrated in her seat. She'd always wanted to visit London and now she was getting to live there for a year. Envisioning red phone booths, glimpses of Will and Kate, and traveling to school on a double decker bus, she fired off a reply with questions of her own.

Just as she was hitting the Send button, another thought pushed the tea and crumpets imagery to the side.

Why am I starting something with Grant when I'm leaving in three months?

A knock at her back door got her feet moving. "I wasn't thinking. That's the problem." She continued the self-talk on the way to the kitchen.

Her belly clenched, as she opened the door to let in the hottest thing to ever set foot in her house. She was beginning to really enjoy that wicked grin of his. To say nothing of the rest of him. His acid washed jeans hung low on his hips. He'd rolled up the cuffs of his white dress shirt that was also open at the collar, revealing just enough of his pecs to get her blood pumping.

She'd barely gotten the door closed behind him when he clasped her by the wrist and pulled her hard against him. Strong arms fenced her as he murmured low in her ear. “Good morning, beautiful.” He tilted her head back and claimed her mouth hard and hungry.

That’s how she’d gone from “this isn’t a good idea” to “kiss me, please?” Like water wore down rock and wind toppled oaks, Grant was an irresistible force of nature. Abby eased her arms around his waist and breathed in the heady scent of his aftershave as she buried her face into his chest.

His kisses trailed tantalizingly slow across her jaw and when he brushed back her hair and began devouring her neck, she thought she’d go up in flames. She tried not to pant as his mouth moved down to her collarbone but gave up when he began to nip at her skin.

“Damn, woman, you taste good.”

She needed to either stop him now or let him take her on her freshly mopped floor. She pushed against the hard plain of his chest without budging him. “Grant, stop.”

He pegged her with a look that asked if that was what she really wanted before loosening his grip on her.

“Good morning to you, too.” She slipped out of his arms and moved to the coffee pot, trying to give her a moment to collect her wits. “Wants some?”

Grant shook his head with a grin. “I’m plenty awake.” He took a deep breath then surveyed her kitchen. His brow furrowed. “Smells like paint, furniture polish, and chocolate chip cookies in here.” He crossed the small room in one long legged stride, hooking his fingers into the belt loops of her jeans to pull her into him again. “Something keeping you awake?”

A smile pulled at the edges of her lips at his

naughty suggestion. Despite his having loved her into a state of relaxed bliss, once in her own bed she'd slept fitfully and woken early. "A couple."

His megawatt smile dimmed. "Tell me."

She shook her head. "Just stuff. School, chores that need doing…"

He tilted her chin up, his blue eyes softening to the color of worn denim. "Us?"

Her stomach did a backwards flip. "Yes."

He brushed his thumb over her cheek before kissing her lightly on the lips. "Me, too." Suddenly, the megawatt smile was back. "I needed a six-mile run this morning, followed by a very long, very cold shower."

The return of Mr. Sex-on-Legs eased her worries. Maybe what he'd said last night pinged around in his head as well. She didn't regret making love to him, but she wasn't ready to think long term either. Standing on tiptoe, she gave him a quick peck back. "I think what the two of us need this morning is to keep busy. The mall should be open by now."

With Grant on her heels, she grabbed her coat and stepped outside. After locking up, she turned to see a pearl colored sedan. "How many automobiles do you have? I don't think I've seen you drive the same thing twice."

Grant opened her door, holding her hand so she could ease into the low-slung auto. "Four." He answered as if everyone in the world had a fleet of planes, trains, and automobiles at their disposal. "I don't drive this one much, but I thought you'd be more comfortable than riding in my truck."

She took in the chrome and wood dash as he moved around the hood. His door barely made a sound as he closed it and when he started the engine, she could barely hear it either.

He pressed a button on the dash and her seat warmed beneath her. “Hmmm. It’s like sitting on a hot, buttered biscuit.” She ran her hand along the blond leather. “This is beautiful. Are you going to be okay carrying around paint cans and brushes?”

He looked over his shoulder and shrugged as they backed out of her drive and onto the street. “It’ll be fine in the trunk.”

They rode in comfortable silence, his thumb skating across the back of her hand until they reached the highway. The four-lane road was nearly empty and he eased the car into the far-left lane and opened the throttle. In a pair of seconds, they were doing the speed limit and then some. He cut his eyes at her. “Why don’t we have Katie and Jackson meet us for lunch?”

Her eyes widened. It was way too soon for that. “I don’t think that’s a good idea.”

“Because?”

This would be so much easier if they weren’t barreling down the highway. She squeezed his hand and hoped she could find the words to explain something she was still trying to wrap her head around. “I’m not ready to go public.”

Grant took his hand off hers to grip the steering wheel with both hands. He turned to her, his face a cross between anger and hurt. “Are you embarrassed about us?”

“Oh goodness, no. I’m dying to talk to Chris.”

A wry smile softened his hurt expression. ““‘I’m crazy about you. If it were up to me, I’d be sending out mass-mailings.”

Her heart thumped against her chest for more than just the fact they were barreling down the road and his attention was on her and not on the cars in front of them. She pointed to the semi they were rapidly closing in on. "Watch the road, please."

Grant whipped the wheel to the left. She let out a breath. "Can we keep this between the two of us for now? I want us to figure this out on our own without our family putting in their two cents worth."

He examined her from the corner of his eye. "You're very logical when it comes to romance, aren't you?"

She shrugged. He made her sound cold, but her cautiousness was born more from experience than logic. "I guess." Thoughts of a couple relationships she wished no one knew about surfaced. Deception on the man's part. Regret on hers. Judgement from family.

With her mind fixed on the past, she wasn't tuned to things outside the car until she caught a glimpse of the mall as they sped past. "You missed the exit."

"We're making a detour first." He looked over his shoulder for traffic and slipped the car into the right lane. At the next exit they pulled off and headed north on Peachtree Industrial. Only then did Grant slow down to a semi-legal speed. The wicked grin made a return appearance as they turned into a luxury auto dealership.

Boys and their toys.

Abby didn't even try not to gawk as they passed row after row of impressive sedans and coupes. She thought about the car she'd drive until the wheels fell off. Grant lived in a whole different world than she. "I can wait in the car if you're not going to be long."

Grant killed the engine and turned up the power on

his smile. “It will make picking out your new car awfully difficult if you do.”

Chapter Twelve

"You have lost your ever-lovin' mind." Not only did he live in another world, but he was also losing touch with the one the other ninety-nine percent of humanity lived in. She shook her head wondering what the monthly payment would be. "I couldn't even afford the tires on one of these cars."

His grin never wavered during her tirade. When she finished, he took both her hands in his and pressed kisses against them. He waited, his expression calm, until she finished. "It's okay, darling. I'm buying it for you."

Abby's jaw went slack. They'd had made love one time and he thought he needed to buy her a car. Didn't that make her a kept woman? An uglier word popped into her head. Mistress. She pulled her hands away, crossing her arms. "That's the stupidest thing I've heard in a long while. I have a perfectly good car."

His smile evaporated and he cocked an eyebrow as he retorted, "Perfectly good, huh? How are you getting to work Monday?"

Abby clenched her jaw. It's okay for him to be logical. "I don't know. I'll figure something out."

As if she hadn't said a word, Grant exited the car, walking around to her door. He opened it and tugged her to her feet. Before she had a chance to put the brakes on the speeding train she was riding, a bright-eyed salesman in a badly fitted suit approached. "What can I show you two this morning?"

"Nothing. He was only looking." She smiled sweetly then took several steps away from the two men.

Still ignoring her, Grant told the salesman, "I want to see what you have in a sedan."

Mr. Bright Eyes beamed. "I have three to choose from." He turned to Abby. "What color did you have in mind?"

This was getting way out of hand. She stalked back to Grant, pulling him out of earshot. "Are you crazy?" She pegged him with a look that had been known to cause hardened ten-year-olds to quake. "Do you have any idea how much those cost?"

He blinked, his face impassive. "About sixty-thousand depending on the upgrades."

"That's more than I make in a year." Her words came out as a hiss. Abby looked at the salesman, offering an apology. "Perhaps you could give us a minute."

Mr. Bright Eyes smiled, waving them off. "Don't worry, husbands and wives argue all the time over cars. I'll let you two talk amongst yourselves."

He thinks we're married?

Abby blinked at the man as he walked towards the showroom then turned to stare at the epitome of All-American handsome. Her morning grew more surreal by the second.

Grant suddenly pulled her into his arms and lifted her chin. His blue eyes darkened to midnight. "I want to take care of you."

She couldn't miss the determination in his voice, or the glare that had turned her smiling Sex-On-Legs into a scowling warrior. Abby swallowed hard.

So much for taking things slow or giving me space. This is a full- scale invasion.

"I take care of myself." She ran her fingers through his hair to take the sting out of her words.

Heat flashed in his blue eyes and the wicked grin returned. "I can be very persuasive."

Her breath caught and everything below her navel roared to life.

Yes, he can.

However, a new car was a bridge too far. "I can be very stubborn," She flashed a grin. "And I've had several more years practice than you."

Seconds ticked by while they stood in the parking lot, neither willing to bend but also not wanting to hurt the other. She saw it in his eyes, the internal battle he waged. He only wanted to see that she was okay. Finally, his blue eyes softened to the shade she loved so much. He stroked her cheek. "Okay, you win."

Abby sensed they'd only declared a truce and she made a move towards his car before he changed his mind. He stilled her hand as she reached for the door handle. "At least let me do this much for you." His voice came out dark and slow like molasses on a January morning.

Yes indeed, he can be mighty persuasive.

She nodded, finding words impossible with his hand skating the length of her back as he eased her inside.

Persuasive or not, she couldn't let him swoop in and start fixing all her problems any more than she could let herself grow accustomed to his help. Since childhood, her only safety net was careful planning and cautious decisions.

Once behind the wheel, he turned to her. "Where are we headed next?" Tension tightened his jaw, making his smile strained.

"The Avenues." Hopefully, the next leg of their shopping misadventure would be riddled with fewer emotional potholes.

An hour and four stores later, Abby handed off the shopping bag to Grant as they left Party Place. She'd given up trying to carry her own bags, figuring she'd won the battle over the car so she could let him have his way about who carried her packages.

As they stepped onto the cobblestone sidewalk of the open-air mall, he pointed to a coffee shop with his chin. "What you say we take a break?"

She checked the people milling around. With churches letting out shortly, the place would soon be a zoo. "We've only been at it an hour."

He pointed to the stores ahead. "Your Sherpa needs a break before we attack the summit."

"Okay, a short one, but then we press on to the end."

Grant guided them passed the open patio filled with Sunday shoppers to a quiet corner inside. "I'll order you something if you want to wait here." He placed the bags in a chair then turned away.

"Skinny latte." Her cheeks ached from smiling. Since leaving the car dealership, Grant had gone out of his way to ease the tension between them. Besides making her laugh at his corny jokes, he'd been careful to keep his public displays of affection to sly touches.

She appreciated his keeping their relationship low key, but she missed his touch. In a short time, she'd come to crave the way his callouses abraded her skin. Her fingers brushed the place on her neck where he'd nipped her, her sensitive skin remembering the searing touch of his mouth.

Maybe if we hurry through the next two stops we can be at his place soon.

"That sneaky rat." His hands-off tactic was working in his favor.

"Someone I know?" He set their orders on the small bistro table. He arched an eyebrow as he handed her the coffee.

Abby patted her cheeks, embarrassed he'd caught her talking to herself. "Never mind me." She blushed further when he shot her a knowing wink.

How can he manage to get me hot and bothered without even being present?

"Before I forget." He pulled the folded receipts from his coat pocket. "Let me give you these." He gestured to the one from the catering supply store. "The kids are going to love the inflatable jump house and slide at the family day picnic, and I was really impressed with the deal you wrangled on the supplies."

"Pinching pennies is one of my many talents." A necessary one considering she wasn't rich as sexy King Midas sitting across from her.

His finger brushed across the back of her hand. "Among others." His voice was low and seductive. Then he shifted around in his seat. Once he'd gotten comfortable, he took a sip from his drink. "I want to thank you again for pitching in with The Help and Hope Foundation. Between the picnic and the new corporate sponsors, you've been working like a fiend. You're going to leave a vacuum when you go to London."

"I'm glad this opportunity came along." Her chest grew tight as she recalled the countdown Ms. Griffin had included in her email.

"When did you decide about the teacher exchange program? You didn't mention it when we were in Turks and Caicos."

"It wasn't until after the wedding." Her gaze darted up to him. "In fact, you should get credit for me making the decision." "How's that?"

"You asked me to go scuba diving with you, and I said I'd be too scared to do it."

The corners of his mouth turned up. "I remember. You got mad and told me to stop bullying you."

Abby shook her head. "You weren't bullying me, just offering me a challenge." She'd been so mad with herself for missing out on an opportunity to do something different that she'd almost signed up for scuba classes her gym offered.

Then she'd run across a flier stuck to the bulletin board in the teachers' lounge. She'd gotten her application in just under the wire. "After years of doing the same thing, I'm ready to shake things up a little. I saw the program not only as a professional challenge but a personal one as well."

"I don't deserve credit for you taking that step." He winked. "You're braver than you think."

"Maybe." She warmed with his praise. "Are you ready to go?"

"How many more stores?" he asked, rocking the male stereotypical attitude on shopping.

"What happened to, 'I'll hold your purse.'?"

He leaned in and whispered. "That was when I thought there was a chance to see you naked."

She rolled her eyes. "One more here at the Avenues, and then we tackle the hardware store."

Grant picked up the pace as they cleared the coffee shop. "Come on then. I actually like hardware stores."

"You'll really like this place. I've been going to Milton Hardware since I bought my house. I'm practically an employee."

Two stores down from their bath store destination, a display outside Mayer's jewelry store stopped her forward momentum. "Oh look, aquamarines," she breathed, touching the glass display case. "So pretty."

Grant quirked an eyebrow. "You like them?"

Were they back to this again?

She cut her eyes at him in warning, to which he quickly raised his hands in surrender. "I do." Humor filled her voice.

"Your birthstone?"

She stepped away from the display. "The last birthday cake Chris made for me had so many candles on it that it looked like the burning of Atlanta." Abby fixed him with one of her famous quelling looks. "Don't laugh. It's true."

He looked at her in mock horror. "Not for all the motorcycles in the world."

The buzz of his phone cut off their laughter, and as he reached for it she pointed to the bedding store. He nodded, thumbing towards the parking lot and they went their separate ways.

Knowing exactly what she wanted, she made it through the store in near record time, meeting Grant just as he was coming in. "All done."

"Excellent." He rubbed his hands together.

"One more store and we can call this day a

success."

****

Grant used to like hardware stores. He could get lost for hours checking out the newest power tools and barbeque grills. As he stood next to Abby in Milton Hardware he decided not anymore, now he hated them. Thanks to the sucker standing behind the paint counter.

The one who couldn't get the lid back on the paint can for staring at her breasts.

"So what room are you painting this girly shade of purple?" the guy with Henry stitched on his shirt asked.

Hardware Henry couldn't have been any more obvious with his leering if he'd had cartoon eyes bugging out of his head. Grant wanted to adjust where the guy's gaze landed with a fist to the jaw. Instead, he wrapped an arm around Abby's shoulders, pulling her in close.

Her brow furrowed, Abby cut her eyes at him, before answering. "I'm redoing Jackson's bedroom. I'll be having some people stay in my home this summer and they have two little girls I thought might like this color."

The explanation pulled Grant from his plans for teaching Hardware Henry some manners. He wanted to talk her out of going, but had no right. They hadn't even talked about being exclusive, much less what they'd do when she left. From his side of the paint counter, Grant knew what he wanted from the relationship. He wanted to throw Abby over his shoulder and bolt out of the store. Grant sucked in a breath, trying to get a handle on his inner caveman. But Hardware Henry was triggering all kinds of possessive instincts.

"Here you go, Abby. I threw in a plastic drop cloth and a couple extra paint stirrers for you." He touched her hand as he passed the supplies to her.

"Awww, Henry. You didn't have to do that. You spoil me," she drawled.

Through his testosterone fog, he noted Abby had quickly snatched her hand away. But Hardware Henry seemed set on acting completely clueless. "Anything for you sweetheart." His lips formed a leering smile as he addressed Abby's chest. "If you have any problems, feel free to call here at the store. I'd be glad to come lend a hand."

Abby's broad smile evaporated. "I think I can handle it."

The sucker opened his mouth like he was going to hit her up with another round of helpfulness. Grant was all over it and leaning over the counter he put it in terms even an idiot could understand. "The lady said she could handle it."

Hardware Henry took a big step backwards. "Sss sure, ri right. Austin can check you out up front."

Grant steered Abby towards the front of the store, his hand resting at the small of her back. But, as they reached the front of the store, Grant saw his trials weren't over. The barely out of his teens guy behind the counter took one look at Abby and brightened like he'd just seen his first Corvette. "Hi, Abby, I haven't seen you here in a while."

"Shame on me, huh." Abby cocked her head, studying the young guy. "Are you growing a beard or did you lose your razor?"

The kid turned bright red from the collar of his shirt to the scalp beneath his brush cut. "Just decided not to shave during my break from school."

"Adds five years to you." She nodded then turned to Grant. "Austin attends Lee Military College." She looked back at the young guy who was still blushing as he bagged Abby's purchases. "Majoring in political science, isn't it?"

"Yes, ma'am." His gaze ping-ponged between Abby and Grant. Then as Grant made eye contact, the kid looked down and away.

That's right, little man.

As much as Grant wanted to cut the kid some slack, he'd run out of understanding and was past ready to get out of the leach-infested place. "Are we done here?" Grant snatched the bags off the counter.

Abby shot him a look that probably caused miscreant ten-year-olds to quake in their sneakers, a look Grant completely earned. "Very done."

His hand firmly around her waist, Grant led them out of the store.

G*od, this had been a long day.*

His palms itched to take Abby in his arms and tell her how crazy he was about her. No, crazy didn't quite get it. He'd left crazy a long time ago. Grant thought back to the only other serious relationship he'd had. The one that had resulted in his beautiful daughter, but thanks in no small part to him had blown up in his face.

Grant slammed the trunk closed and raked his fingers threw his hair. He wanted this thing with Abby to go somewhere, but he if wanted it, he was going to have to drop the steamer trunks worth of baggage he was humping. The memory of walking in on his wife flashed in his head. Whatever it took, he'd do just about anything to never have a repeat of that.

He reached for the ignition. "Would you like me to pick us up some lunch before we head back to your place?" Gunning the engine, he pulled out of the Milton Hardware like he'd just boosted the thing, like if he drove fast enough he could outrun the past.

Abby drummed her fingers against the door handle. "Just take me home."

While moving the sedan through Sunday afternoon traffic, he cut his eyes at her. "You're awfully quiet." She chuffed, thinking he really didn't want her talking right now. After another few minutes of silence, during which the thrumming in her head only got louder, she had to let some of her anger out. Either that or her head was going to explode. "You know, I wasn't planning on running off with Henry."

He nodded but didn't offer an explanation.

Abby rolled her eyes. "Your hands were all over me the whole time we were in his department. Same goes for Austin in check out. If you'd have felt me up any more, we'd have gotten kicked out." She didn't mind public displays of affection if they were for the right reasons. Marking his territory wasn't a valid reason.

He scowled at her from beneath hooded eyes that turned the color of midnight. "They were undressing you with their eyes."

Abby barked out a laugh but not because she thought anything about the situation was humorous. "No, they weren't. They were flirting. I'm a longtime customer. That's all. I'm not interested in them."

"All you would have had to do was crook your finger and both those men would have been all over you like a bad suit. I know because you have the same effect on me."

His comment might have made her hot and bothered if she wasn't mad at him. "And you think I'm just going to have sex with the first guy who winks at me or gives me an extra paint stick." She was really feeling a head of steam rolling. "Is it my moral character in question here or womankind universally?"

Grant steered the car into a grocery store parking lot. After killing the engine, he let out a breath. "Dang. This is so not how I saw this day going. I don't want to fight with you again."

She jutted out her chin. "Don't be an ass and that won't be a problem. I don't appreciate that you've felt the need to stake your claim."

Faster than she could track, he had her seatbelt off and was tugging her across the center console and into his lap. She really wanted to dig in her heels. Now was not the time to manhandle her.

He cupped her face gently in his huge hands. Below the three worry lines creasing his forehead, his crystal blue eyes were pleading. "I have some bad history with infidelity, so I'm probably hypersensitive about flirting."

Her anger melted. "Is that why you asked if Chris and I were a couple?

He nodded, closing his eyes. When he opened them after a couple seconds, they were the color of the sea after a storm. "Listen, don't judge Heather because what happened was my fault too. She had an affair after we had Grace. In retrospect if I'd paid more attention to her, she wouldn't have sought comfort with someone else. She needed something and I wasn't giving it to her. She found someone who would."

That explains a truckload of his behavior.

It also put her in a bind. Did she want to risk reciprocating with her own truth? She took a deep breath, hoping he'd offer her the same level of understanding as he did his ex-wife. "I can't judge Heather because I've been there and done that."

His eyes widened as if she'd slapped him, but he needed to hear this. She twined her fingers with his. "Jackson's father was one of my dance instructors at Julliard. I knew he was married but I believed him when he told me he was divorcing his wife." She closed her eyes as the memory of that ugly, but long-ago scene played in her mind. "He started singing a different tune when I told him he'd gotten me pregnant." She opened her eyes to Grant's compassionate face.

"That's different. You were young, and he took advantage of your innocence. Heather knew what she was doing."

She shook her head. "Emotions can really cloud people's judgment and experience doesn't always help. If it did, it would have helped me tune into the fact that the last guy I dated wasn't being honest with me."

"Married?"

"Believe me, the second I found out I sent his sorry butt packing. My integrity is an important part of who I am." She clenched his fingers, willing him to hear and believe. "As long as I'm with you, there will only be you."

Grant let out a breath. "Now it's you who knows the exact thing to say." Then he grinned down at her. "That goes for me as well. Now that we've got that settled, can I buy the car to make up for my stupidity?"

“No, but you can take me back to your place, and I’ll let you find another way of making this up to me.”

Chapter Thirteen

Grant squeezed Abby's hand. "I feel sure this day has turned out to be far more of an adventure than you expected. Why don't you close your eyes and relax for a few minutes?"

It would take more than soft music and a warm behind for her to relax. He pulled onto Georgia 400 and they rode the dozen miles between the mall and his place in silence.

Things changed once he had them inside his cottage. Before she could take more than a step inside, he took her hard against the nearest wall. "I need you." His words came out as a low rumble. "I need to know we're okay, to hold on to you for a while."

She breathed in deeply, willing herself to forget the past couple hours. The scent of sandalwood filled her head and the rasp of his whiskers against her skin brought back luscious memories of yesterday. Putting their issues aside proved harder than Grant's firm embrace.

"Me too." The weight of the past pressed against her. The future wasn't feather light either. She clenched her fist by her side as he continued to feather kisses down to her collarbone.

He pulled back to look at her. His mouth turned up in a grin that revealed one of his dimples. "I think what you need is a glass of wine and a back rub."

She leaned into his body, determined not to let their problems steal what she had right in front of her. "That sounds wonderful. When you've got my shoulders down from around my ears, then you can have your wicked way with me."

Grant guided her over to his sofa then began tugging off her flats. He finished by drawing her legs up so she was reclining and handed her the remote. "Why don't you pick us out a movie for later while I open a bottle of wine?"

Abby flipped through the choices available on his on-line account as she scanned his living room. When she'd been there the night before, she'd been too preoccupied with his ministrations to notice his much about the cottage. The best thing she decided after checking out the huge wall mounted monitor and ugly recliner was the soft leather sofa she was curled up on. She pulled a chocolate-colored blanket off the back of the sofa and sank deeper into its softness.

After a few minutes he returned, a pair of large wine glasses cupped in one hand. He handed one to her before slipping under the blanket and waggled his eyebrows. "Relaxed yet?"

"Getting there." Abby brought the glass to her lips to hide her silly grin. Against his charm, she was a crayon left in the sun. She took another sip then set her glass on the coffee table. "Which would you prefer, action or comedy?" Likely one of the two categories was a good bet.

He took the remote and clicked on the first choice he came to, a documentary on ancient Egypt. Then his hands tunneled under the blanket to travel the length of her body. "Doesn't matter, the movie is just an excuse to make out for a couple hours." He pressed her down to the sofa with his body and began torturing her earlobe with tiny nibbles.

With every inch of her skin between her neck and her shoulders attended to, he kissed his way across her cheek. As his lips touched hers, his kisses became urgent, conveying his desire for her better than the sweetest words. He licked at the seam of her mouth and she eagerly opened for him. His tongue caressed her own, igniting a firestorm of lust that threatened to consume her.

Finally, she could take no more and pushed against his shoulder. Her breaths came in hectic pants, making her feel as though she'd been dancing for hours instead of only their tongues doing the tango. "What are we, a couple teenagers?"

He sat up, pulling her with him. "I feel like one when I'm with you. Now that I've finally gotten to make love to you, it's all I can think of."

"I'm glad I have that effect on you." She slid his hand under the collar of her blouse so he could feel her heart pounding. "Since this is what you do to me."

The corners of his mouth turned up. "I was beginning to think I was never going to get past your defenses. The Pentagon could take lessons from you."

He looked at her from beneath hooded eyes. His cobalt blue eyes and the feel of his fingers against her sensitive flesh set off a chain reaction. Her nipples pebbled and desire uncurled in her belly. Abby shook her head. "I can't seem to remember why I ever thought this was a bad idea."

Grant leaned in until their foreheads met. His voice was a deep purr. "I know I promised you a back rub, but I have a better idea." He combed his fingers through her hair then stood. "I'll just be a couple minutes."

The sound of water piqued her curiosity and had her on her feet. She followed her ears through his bedroom until she found him in a white-tiled bath. The marble countertops and double sink barely registered considering the Olympic sized bathtub.

Grant turned when she entered, spreading his arm over the jetted tub. "I don't have any candles or fancy bath oil."

Abby sat on the platform surrounding the tub and trailed her fingers through the foaming water. "This is perfect."

Gone was his playful banter, replaced with a scowl that made him seem more warrior than lover. He tugged her to her feet and began roughly working the buttons of her blouse. When he'd finished, he pulled it from her shoulders and slipped his hands over her stomach to begin stripping off her jeans. Still on his knees, he hooked his fingers under her panties and eased them down her hips.

"The water's ready. Get in." Grant held out his hand while she stepped into the hot water.

"That feels good," she groaned, closing her eyes.

"Scoot up," he commanded.

He eased in behind her, urging her to use him as a pillow once he'd settled in the water. She tilted her neck in invitation, loving the way he nuzzled the soft spot behind her ear.

Grant breathed in deeply. "You smell like heaven."

Abby sank into his embrace. "You're right. This is better than just a back rub. I'm going to stay in here until I get pruney."

His chest moved against her back as he chuckled. "How long does that usually take?"

"Hmm," she groaned. "Hours."

"I've got forever," he murmured in her ear.

After they made love, she let out a slow breath. "Mission accomplished. I'm officially relaxed."

They lay in each other's arms, letting the cooling water lap against their bodies. Grant tilted her chin. "I think we better get out. If we get any more relaxed we'll be in danger of drowning."

Sliding from beneath her, Grant stepped out first before pulling Abby to her feet. With one hand he reached for a towel while lifting her from the tub. Then he folded the wide expanse of fluffy cotton around her and scooped her into his arms. "I want you in my bed." He carried her into the other room. After flipping back the comforter, he eased them both onto the bed. "Are you warm enough." He settled the blanket back over them.

She could only nod her response. The fact, he'd loved her to the point she was wordless as well as boneless must have pleased him. Grant let out a very masculine purr and settled his body next to hers. He represented everything she could ever desire in a lover: honest, passionate, and giving.

As they lay spooning each other, unexpected tears formed in Abby's eyes. *Oh God!* As the salty droplets slipped down her cheeks, she realized she was falling in love with Grant. She brushed them away. Now was not the time to ponder the depth of her feelings for him or worry about what they'd do when she left for London. They had this moment and that was all anyone was guaranteed.

Grant drew her closer. “Is it okay that I want you again?”

“More than okay,” she chuckled.

“I never knew I could need someone so much.” They lay together, him trailing a lazy hand over her hip. “Penny for your thoughts.”

Several seconds passed in silence. “I’m wondering if I wanted to risk starting another argument with you.”

Her imagination shot to the land minds they tripped that afternoon. “Better have it out.”

A faint smile played at his lips. “This is not a birthday present since you don’t have those.” He reached to the nightstand and pulled out a rectangular, black velvet box.

Her fingers trembled as she pried open the lid. A line of magnificent blue stones set in delicate white gold twinkled up at her. Taking her hand, he fixed the bracelet to her wrist. “You can call it an apology for my behavior earlier.”

She turned her wrist so the stones caught the light. “It’s spectacular.”

“You like it?”

“I love it. You didn’t have to do that.”

A grin softened his chiseled features. He clutched her hands, turning them over to press kisses into her palm. “I know, but I wanted to.” When he looked up his eyes sparked. “I hope when you wear it you’ll remember that you mean a great deal to me.”

“Always.” The stones reminded her of his eyes, light blue but with a fire emanating from deep within.

He tucked her into his body and relaxed. But for hours afterward, Abby marked the passage of time by watching the light outside Grant’s bedroom window faded from gold to pink to grey. He'd drifted to sleep and while he'd driven her body beyond the point of ecstasy, she had too many things on her mind to sleep. All the drama they'd been through, made their love making feel like a sweet victory. But her newly discovered feelings for him terrified her. How did people make love to one another and not give their hearts away? She concluded her friends who claimed to be able to do it were either lying or had never made love the way she and Grant did.

She rested her cheek against the hard plane of his chest and listened to his shallow, even breaths. All she wanted from the rest of this day was a few more minutes with him. Instead, she kissed the underside of his jaw. "Wake up. I need you to drive me home."

He wrapped his heavy arm around her and kissed the top of her head. "I have a better idea. How about I drive you to work in the morning?"

Oh God, that is so tempting.

Abby forced herself to sit up. "I can't. I need fresh clothes." She scooted off the bed as he made a move for her. Abby slipped into the bathroom to retrieve her clothes, with Grant hot on her heels. He leaned against the sink and watched as she collected her scattered clothes, arms folded across his broad chest and a leer on his lips. When she'd finished dressing he reached for his, sliding jeans over his bare butt in a slow, sensual way that made her second guess her decision to leave.

He tugged a set of keys from his pocket and took her hand. "Compromise." His blue eyes sparked like the blue stones she wore on her wrist. "Take my car."

She rolled her eyes. "Was that your plan all along? Fake me out with one outrageous car so later I'd accept an only slightly less outrageous one. "

He pulled her in close and tilted her head back. "I wish I was that clever."

Palming the keys, she growled. "It's just until mine gets fixed."

He shrugged, "Of course." then reached around to squeeze her bottom. "But I think after those cute buns of yours are all warm and toasty in the morning you're going to rethink your stance."

"We'll see."

"I'll call you during my layovers this week."

Abby clenched her eyes. Five days without seeing him shouldn't seem like such a long time. Hiding her feelings behind sassy words she winked. "Sure, and when you get back we'll need to spend more time in your tub?"

Grant cocked an eyebrow, a wolf-grin forming on his lips. "Heck, yeah." He devoured her mouth.

She breathed in his intoxicating scent one more time before easing from his arms. "I better go because if you do that much longer, I'll have to explain to my principal why I'm wearing jeans on a Monday."

Chapter Fourteen

The air traffic controller's voice came in over Grant's headset in a squawk. "Five-Nine-Four Romeo Charlie, you're clear to land on runway two-six."

"Roger that, tower. Cleared to land Runway two-six, five-nine-four Romeo-Charlie." He pushed the throttle forward on the jet on its final approach into Peachtree-DeKalb Airport.

After delivering several cases of shrimp to a five-star restaurant in Wisconsin, he'd picked up another haul from Madison over to Butte, Montana. At the rate his company was growing it would clear ten million this year. The financial success came with a price. It had been a hard five days filled with long flights, bad food, and little rest. To say nothing of how badly he'd missed Abby. Phone calls and texts, as sexy as they'd been, were a poor substitute for the real thing.

He landed the twin-engine turbo prop right on the numbers then taxied to the Davis Air Transport hanger. Twenty minutes later, as the sun was beginning to peek over the horizon, he was heading north on I-85. At that hour there wasn't another soul on the road so he leaned over the handlebars and opened the throttle of his bike. Most of the stuff he owned was just that, stuff. Not points of pride or possessions to impress. But God, he loved this machine. It was like riding a jet engine bareback. Finally, he slowed the machine below the hundred mile-an-hour mark, eased off the highway, and into the parking lot of Northland Motorsports.

He powered his machine up to the front door just as a raw-boned fifty-something man exited through the front doors of the store. Frank Wilson, a customer of Davis Air-Transport and owner of the store, stepped to a massive example of American craftsmanship and patted the brushed chrome fuel tank. "What do you think?"

Grant looked over the touring bike. Any part that hadn't been chromed-out had been painted a high-gloss black. It also had black leather saddlebags, a backrest, and a place for the passenger to her feet. It wasn't what he'd pick if it were just himself. He liked the sleek lines and crazy-ass speed of his baby. "I think it'll get the job done." If this worked out the way he hoped he might consider buying her. "Did the jacket and helmet I ordered come in?"

Frank thumbed over his shoulder to the bike. "Yep, I just stowed them in the saddle bags right there. Sally also threw in something for you for the road."

Grant's face broke into a broad grin. Sally and Frank were good people. When Grant had called them up with the idea to trade machines for the weekend they'd at first been a little unsure. Sally didn't like the idea of Frank getting on what she'd called "a Darwin Award machine." Then he told her what he wanted the bike for. "Tell Sally thanks for me." He tossed the man the keys to his machine. "Don't get into too much trouble on my ride. She's pretty but unforgiving."

Frank returned his grin. "Sounds like a woman I once knew."

"I'll bring this back on Monday." He pulled on his

helmet. Then he took off down the road to push a certain someone a little further from her comfort zone.

He pulled into Abby's driveway and killed the engine. Briefly, he considered giving her a heads up, but that would've given her time to create a couple dozen excuses. Stealth was what he needed for this mission. He stepped up to her back door and gave it a firm pounding. This early on a Saturday morning she was probably still asleep. He gave her a minute then hit the door again.

Abby jerked the thing open like she was gunning for whoever was on the other side. She wore a pair of blue plaid sleep-pants and a white tank-top that clung perfectly to her breast. In the glow of the overhead light she'd flipped on, he could clearly see the darkened shadow of her nipples through the fabric. It took her a second but then she smiled shyly, ducked her chin, and stepped back to let him in. "When did you get back?" Her voice came out gravelly with sleep and sexy as hell.

For a moment he considered taking her back to bed. He closed in on her, wrapping his arms around her waist and burying his face in her bed-tousled hair. "About an hour ago." This was what he'd been after when he'd pushed the limits of the jet, something far better than a good meal and a warm bed. His version of heaven had the prettiest pair of whiskey eyes and curls a man could get lost in. He kissed her on the temple then reluctantly let her go, telling himself to stick to the plan.

She ran her fingers through her hair trying to tame the golden-blond curls. "Did you want some coffee?"

"That'd be great."

She turned to the counter behind her and began going through the motions of filling the carafe and spooning the coffee. Even her rearview was beautiful. He slipped behind her and after kissing his way up her neck, he teased her earlobe with tiny nibbles. "I missed you."

She tilted her head giving him better access and leaned back into his chest. "Me too."

Grant saw himself pushing his hands up through the bottom of her tank top to palm the tempting swells of her breast. He kissed the sweet spot behind her ear then forced himself to back off. Swatting her playfully on the behind, he barked, "Go get dressed. I've got a surprise for you."

She folded her arms across her chest, looking stubborn and sexy since her arms had pushed her breast distractingly upwards. "Like what?" Her eyes narrowed. "I'm not going to need a harness and a parachute for this surprise."

"Would I do that to you?" He attempted to sound innocent. Then he pointed in the direction of her bedroom. "Jeans and a long-sleeve t-shirt will be fine."

When she returned fifteen minutes later, he looked her over. She'd taken his wardrobe suggestion and also pulled her hair back into a low ponytail. "Do you have anything sturdier than those?" He pointed to the lightweight sneakers.

She cocked her head at him, suspicion lacing her voice. "I have a pair of hiking boots."

"Perfect."

She returned, wearing the boots. Holding her arms out, she turned for him to see. "Will I do now?"

The light brown t-shirt brought out the caramel

color in her hair and her low-slung jeans hung at just the right spot on her hips. He couldn't resist and crossed the kitchen in a pair of strides to take her in his arms. Looking down at her he announced, "You'll more than do." Then after a quick kiss he tugged her arm. "Come, we have a full day ahead of us."

Grant moved through the door first, strategically placing his body between her and the bike. Once she'd locked the door and stowed the keys in her purse, he stepped aside. Her eyes shot to the bike, growing wide as understanding set in. Then they darted to him. Her lips pressed together for a moment before she hitched the strap of her purse onto her shoulder and turned on her heels.

He caught her as she reached for the doorknob. "Come on honey, give it a try. It will be fun. I promise."

She spun around and glared. "Can you also promise I won't end up a splattered mess on the road?"

He snaked one hand around her waist and with the other he tilted her chin. Her normally warm, chocolate eyes were nearly black with fear. "I can't. I can't promise that you won't get t-boned by a semi on the way to work Monday, catch your death of cold, or get skin cancer either." He kissed the end of her nose. "But I've made this as safe as possible."

He held her until the tension melted from her body. Then he took her by the hand and drew her slowly to the bike, much as one would introduce a child to a Great Dane. Letting go of her, he unlatched one of the saddle bags, taking out a fitted leather jacket and holding it up for her to see.

"I bought this especially for you." He opened the

front of the coat and fingered the black mesh lining. "See this. There are metal plates underneath." He patted the chrome helmet strapped to the back of the bike. "Plus this." He brushed his thumb across her cheek. "Do you really think I'd ask you to do this if I thought it was truly dangerous?"

She gave him a hard stare before finally letting out her breath. "No."

Her admission brought a smile to his lips. "We'll take it up the street and if you still don't like it, we won't go."

"Promise?"

He traced an X over his chest. "Cross my heart."

She swatted his arm then grabbed the jacket. After shrugging it on and pulling up the zipper, she pointed a finger at him. "I'm keeping the jacket regardless. It's cute."

Grant unstrapped her helmet from its spot behind her backrest. "I wouldn't have it any other way," he told her, then pulled it over her head and fixed the chinstrap.

He did the same with his own helmet, watching with growing admiration as she mounted the bike without any further coaxing. He spoke into the helmets' integrated communication system. "Can you hear me now?"

She flashed a surprised smile. "Yes."

He pointed back to the footrest. "Your feet go here." Abby placed her feet on the metal runner and he threw a leg over the bike. She clenched his biceps. "Can I hold on to you?"

He eased her hands down to the tops of his hips. "Of course, that's the best part," he assured her then started the engine. In an instant her arms became steal bands around his middle.

"How you doing back there?" He hoped she'd at least give them to the end of the street.

Her voice came out high and reedy. "Um, okay I guess."

Easing the throttle forward, he moved them smoothly up her street and on to Scott Boulevard. Her death grip hadn't lessened, but she also wasn't screaming at him to turn around either, so he took a chance and made a right turn on to Clairmont Avenue. When the sign for I-85 south came into view he asked, "What'll it be?"

Dead air hung between them for a second. Her voice quivered when she finally spoke. "Keep going."

As he accelerated the bike onto the on-ramp, she tightened her vice-like grip around his stomach and clenched him between her thighs. The embrace would have been erotic if it didn't mean she was scared as hell. He took his hand off the handlebar long enough to pat her hand for reassurance.

Ten minutes into the ride, the concrete and steel by the side of the road gave way to grass and trees. He slowed the bike so Abby could catch glimpses of a few spring flowers that had started to appear and was rewarded when her death grip eased.

"Look, the daffodils are blooming."

"They're even more the further south we go." He brought the bike's speed down another notch when more of the yellow flowers came into view.

Having in mind some other sights she might enjoy, he was about to sped up when Abby leaned her body onto his and rested her cheek against his back. His pulse kicked into overdrive as if the two of them were barreling down the highway instead of ambling down the road. The trust her embrace implied ripped through his chest.

Then she slid her hands down his thighs. Every time he thought he'd figured this woman out, she did something that completely threw him for a loop. Hell, she was turning their ride into foreplay. He shifted on the seat trying to make an unobtrusive adjustment as his erection turned to stone.

Below the little town of Fairburn, Grant eased the bike off the interstate and onto a two-lane blacktop. Man, he loved the hairpin turns of north Georgia, but the middle of the state had its own share of curves and rolling hills. He resisted the urge to open of the throttle and lean into the next curve. Why mess with a good thing? Abby's bone crushing grip had softened into a gentle embrace that kept him teetering on the edge of comfort and arousal. Grant saw the two of them doing this every weekend for the next twenty years or so.

Quickly, he reined in those long-term images. He was getting way ahead of himself, and apparently, where Abby was as well. Beyond discussing Help and Hope's picnic, any time he mentioned the future, she changed the subject. It was killing him not to bring up her move to London.

From their first kiss, he'd been completely addicted. The kick he got from gazing into her warm eyes or tasting that sweet spot behind her ear was better than any speed induced adrenaline rush. The thoughts of his addiction moving thousands of miles away made him more than a little irrational. More than once he'd thought of asking her not to go.

He gripped the handlebars, knowing what a selfish pig that would make him. He was in love with her, he'd know that for weeks, but what he also had come to realize that beyond lust and passion, he just plain loved her and because of that he wanted what she wanted.

"You ready to stretch your legs?"

"I could stop." Her voice was as smooth as a bottle of twelve-year-old scotch.

Grant eased them off the road by an open field. After Abby slid her leg over the back of the bike, he twisted on the seat to open the far saddlebag. Beneath the folded plaid blanket lay a canvas drawstring bag. "I thought we'd have a picnic."

Abby tugged off her helmet and finger combed her hair. Then when she saw what he had, her lovely face brightened into a wide smile. She reached for the bags and began pulling out sandwiches, drinks, and plastic bags of fruit and sweets. "You thought of everything."

"I had help." He made a mental note to send his friend's wife a big thanks. Wrapping his arm around her waist, he led them up the gentle swells of an open pasture. Surrounded by bright green clover, he flicked the blanket open then tugged her to the ground. He tore into a bag of grapes and popped one into Abby's open mouth. "What do you think?"

She eyed him darkly and inched closer. With a kiss on his jaw she purred, "I think that I've been riding a five-hundred-pound vibrator for the last two hours and I want to make love to you."

Grant looked around at the rolling hills and back over his shoulder to the road. The tips of the handlebars were barely visible from their spot. "Here?"

A wicked grin bloomed on her face. "Sure. Why

not?"

Grant let the bag of grapes fall to the blanket and pulled Abby on top of him. "I think I should have taken you riding weeks ago."

Respectable women did not have sex in wide open fields. For some reason she didn't care what other women did. Since she'd met him, he'd pushed, teased, and cajoled her into taking risks she'd have never considered. Abby wanted to show him just how far she'd come under his tutelage.

He rolled to his side, taking her with him so they faced each other. "You never cease to amaze me." Pressing a gentle kiss to her lips, he began making love to her.

Long moments later when they were both sated, he wrapped his thick arms around her. They lay dozing, their limbs tangled together. "I bet they don't have secluded fields like this one in London."

Abby's heart clenched. "You're probably right, but there are other good things about London. Not as nice as open fields, but important things." She combed her fingers through his hair. "I jumped into adulthood at the deep end, getting pregnant at nineteen. Because of that, I had to make choices based on what was best for Jackson."

Her gaze shot to Grant's." Don't get me wrong, I've loved being his mom and I've had a good life, but I missed out on that part of life where I could follow my own agenda. If I want to do something different, this is the time to do it. In a couple years Katie and Jackson will want to start a family and I'll want to be there for that."

Amid her explanation lay one unspoken question:

What about the two of them?

He leaned up on one elbow, dark emotions playing across his handsome face. "You're right, as usual." His sensual lips slipped into a forced smile. "A front's coming through. We need to get going."

An hour later when Grant pulled into her driveway, having returned her safely just as he promised, she should have felt relief. Instead, tension stiffened her muscles. Abby reached for her keys. "Did you want to come in? I have some leftover chicken casserole I could heat up."

Hemming her against her back door, he shook his head. "All I want right now is a hot shower and a comfortable bed." His hooded eyes left her no doubt where he was hoping to get those things.

She unlocked her door and took a step inside. Her heart began thudding in her chest nearly as rapidly as when she'd first thrown her leg over Grant's bike. "I know what you mean." She trembled, a smile plastered on her face. "I think I've got grass in my underwear." Abby might have become brave enough to ride a motorcycle and make love in an open field, but could she take this step?

Her tiny bungalow symbolized more than home to her. Like a castle's keep, it was her safe retreat, and she guarded the walls with more vigilance than any sentry. She never invited a date inside and had certainly never taken any lover into her bed.

Grant wasn't *any* lover though. With every teasing word and gentle action, he chipped away at her defenses until he'd worked his way into her heart. "You could clean up here if you like then maybe afterward..."

His devilish grin made her glad she was turning into a risk taker. He backed her into the kitchen. After kicking the door closed, he worked the leather jacket he'd given her off her shoulders. Pausing only long enough to tug off their boots, they pealed each other's clothes off on their way to her bath.

They reached the tiny room naked and breathless. "It's not as luxurious as yours." She pointed to the old-fashioned enameled tub. "I'm not even sure we'll both fit." She couldn't ignore the comparison not only between their homes but their financial status as well.

"It's perfect. Besides, I work well in confined spaces." His hand traced the curve of her back.

Desire burned through the remnants of her insecurity. *God,* he had a way of putting her at ease at the same time he kept her on the knife's edge of need. The only thing keeping her from pulling him down to the tile floor was the promise of how good he'd feel beneath her soap slicked fingers.

Abby slipped from his embrace. "Let me get the water going." As she fumbled with the tub's handles, he spooned his body against hers.

"Is it hot enough yet?"

"Any hotter and you might get burned." She matched his innuendo with one of her own. Not only was his daredevil ways rubbing off on her, so was his sultry banter. Watching him from over her shoulder, Abby stepped under the water. His gaze raked over her in an appreciative stare. Feeling bolder than she ever thought possible, she arched her back in a way designed to drive him crazy. He rewarded her efforts with a groan that was quickly followed by the feel of his arms snaking around her body.

They both reached for the soap. "Me first." She tugged it from his fist. After working the bar into lather, she soaped his shoulders, arms, and stomach.

"My turn to play." He took the soap from her. Turning her around, he caressed the sore muscles of her back with the expertise of the best masseur. Then he attended to the rest of her. Finally, he stepped her under the spray. "All done?"

Twisting in his embrace, she brought her lips to his ear. "Not even close" Though she still needed a minute to gather her wits.

After shutting off the water, Grant reached for a towel. He patted her dry, while she clung to his shoulders for support. When he'd wrapped another towel around his waist, he scooped her into his arms and stepped lithely from the tub. So replete from his ministrations, she barely registered the deft way he managed to pull back her satin comforter while still holding her in his arms.

Their bodies came together in a way that seemed as if it had been ages rather than minutes since they'd made love.

Afterward, he collapsed momentarily onto her before rolling them so that they lay facing each other. He brushed her still wet hair from her face and studied her in a tender way that had her clenching her eyes. Too late, she realized inviting him into her bed was the least of her worries. He'd taken up residence in her heart in a way she'd never allowed another man.

Grant kissed her still closed eyes. "I should go before that front catches up with me." He slipped from her bed.

She made a move to join him, but he stilled her

with a hand to her shoulder. “Stay. On my way home, I want to think about you all cozy and warm like that.”

Had he asked, she would have gladly let him see her with tangled hair and puffy eyes in the morning. “Okay.” Still…

It’s not in my best interest to get used to having Grant’s big body filling my bed.

While he was still collecting the clothes they’d scattered throughout the house, a chill had already set in. Abby shivered, telling herself it was only the after effect of her wet hair. At the sound of her back door closing and the roar of his motorcycle that quickly followed, tears sprang to her eyes. She was in so much trouble!

Abby scrubbed them away. “Don’t be such a ninny.”

She bolted from the bed and after grabbing a flannel nightgown from her dresser, stalked to the bathroom to dry her hair. Socks, hot chocolate, and another blanket added to the bed didn’t chase the chill from her. Finally, she resorted to sleeping on the couch in front of a fire.

Sleeping was the wrong word. She didn’t so much sleep, as close her eyes and imagine how good it would have felt if he’d stayed. While they’d returned home without so much as a scratch, it didn’t mean she didn’t wake the next morning feeling more than a little battered. She stretched, trying to work the kinks out of her soar arms and legs, but more than that her heart ached, reminding her bravery had its costs.

Chapter Fifteen

"I want you to meet Grace." Grant announced, after a sultry greeting and a how-was-your-day.

Abby's stomach did a flip. For some single parents "meeting the kids" signaled the next step in the relationship, while others brought their significant others home to meet the kids early on. No sense getting too involved, if he and the kids don't mesh.

"That would be great." Which category did Grant fall into?

"Super." His excitement rumbled through the phone. "Wear comfortable jeans, and old shoes."

"The last time you gave me wardrobe instructions I ended up on the back of a motorcycle. Should I be worried?"

"Depends on how you feel about horses."

"Really?" He'd been so reticent when she first mentioned hippotherapy. "What made you change your mind?"

"I talked it over with Heather and what she said made sense. If Grace is having fun, it doesn't matter that they can't scientifically prove it helps."

"Good for you." Abby once again marveled at Grant and Heather's ability to work through their differences in the name of their daughter's wellbeing.

"Her lesson is at noon. Come here at eleven and we'll go together."

"I'll see you then." She started to hang up. Instead, she blurted out, "I'm looking forward to meeting her." Abby felt she already knew Grace. Katie had been sharing pictures and stories of her niece from the time the little girl was born. Then as Abby and Grant had grown close, she'd heard the more poignant parts of Grace's history. About the milestones missed, the doctors, the diagnosis.

Right on time, Abby waved at the guard as she passed through the gate. With Harvey still on the critical list at the garage, she was driving one of Grant's cars. Her pride had waged war on her sense of practicality, and though the battle had been tough, in the end practicality had won. One thing that helped was getting to breeze through security in his pass-identified car.

Driving through the expensive subdivision, she felt as if she was caught in an episode of *Dallas*. The theme song played in her head as she pulled on to the long drive leading to the house he'd bought for Grace. Thank heavens, the similarities between the Davis clan and the Ewings the ended there.

Instead of parking at the gatehouse, as she did most times, she pulled the car up to the main house. Breathing deeply to settle her nerves, Abby reminded herself not to expect a lot of interaction from Grace. All kinds of professional talk ran through her mind, but her heart wanted this to go well. Abby snagged the Easter basket from the passenger seat and made her way to the front door.

She rang the bell then set the basket down so her hands were free. Usually, Grant had the door open before the chimes finished, and had a habit of pulling her across the threshold into an over the top greeting. Not that she minded. She'd just learned the hard way not to have anything spillable in her hands when he opened the door.

After several seconds, she pushed the bell again, and waited. She was about to fish her cell phone from her purse when Grant finally opened. "Hey, beautiful." He pressed a kiss to her hair. "Sorry about taking so long. I was just finishing packing Grace's bag."

Taking a cue from his less demonstrative greeting, Abby slipped her arm around him in one of those hugs she usually reserved for other women's husbands and boyfriends. The kind where she wasn't pressing her boobs into the guy's chest. "No problem."

Grant led her into a large family room. "Grace, come here, sweetheart. There's someone Daddy wants you to meet."

From the time at Katie and Jackson's wedding when he'd extended his hand and drawled, "Ms. Roberts would you care to dance," she loved the deep way his voice resonated. This gentle coaxing made her heart ache it was so sweet.

A blonde head peeked from behind a wall. "Don't be shy, sugar."

"I brought her a present." Abby held up the basket. Ever the teacher, she'd purchased several board books and art supplies instead of candy.

"You didn't have to do that." His gaze shifted. "She will love you even without it." He fingered one of the books. "But, you're going to have a new best friend with this."

"Katie told me Grace was a dog lover."

At the word, Grace ventured from behind the wall.

What an angel.

Her blond hair was pulled back in a pair of not quite perfect ponytails. She scurried along the wall until she reached Grant's leg, where she promptly tucked herself behind.

Abby bent to one knee. "Hi there, my name's Abby."

A dimpled hand waved from behind her father's leg. "Abby brought you a present." Stepping aside, Grant brushed his hand over her hair. "Tell her thank you."

Abby held the basket out, and her heart warmed as Grace touched her fingers to her lips signing "thank you." Then she immediately plunked herself on the floor and pulled the book from the basket.

"That went okay, didn't it?" The tightness in her chest loosened.

His eyes widened. "Were you worried? I can't imagine a child not liking you."

"I was."

Grant took her hand, and they watched Grace investigate her basket. Then after a few minutes, he checked his watch. "Do you mind keeping an eye on her for a second? I need to grab some things from upstairs."

She shook her head. "Not at all." Abby's hands itched to run her fingers through Grace's hair. "Would you like me to read that to you?"

Grace signed, "yes" and crawled onto the sofa next to Abby.

She took the book and read just as she had to hundreds of children. The act brought her back to Jackson's childhood. It had been years since a little one sat tucked into her side.

"See, I told you she would love you." Grant walked into the room.

The sight of his arms filled with a purple backpack and tiny helmet brought a smile to her lips. "Anything I can do to help?"

"Nope, I've got it. We better hurry or we'll be late."

Twenty minutes later, they were finally pulling out of the garage. Abby tucked her hands beneath her. Her fingers itched to run up his shoulders and along his nape. She'd grown addicted to letting her hands have free range.

"Preflight check out all right?"

"I've got my two best girls in the car with me. Can't be too careful." Grant adjusted the mirrors before pushing the ignition. The sound of *The Wheels on The Bus* filled the air.

A laugh bubbled up. "When I'm a doddering old lady and don't even know my own name, I'll probably still know the lyrics to this song."

He sang a few lines, his deep voice sounding simultaneously fantastic and silly when singing about a never-ending bus ride. "They kinda get in your head, don't they?"

With the music filling the SUV's interior, they reached the stables. Rocks pinged against the underside of Grant's vehicle as he drove up the rutted, narrow drive leading from the highway to McCracken's Farm.

After taking Grace from her car seat, Grant held on to her hand as she tugged him towards the riding rink.

Abby hung back, letting him do the daddy thing until it came time for Grant to relinquish Grace to the care of the therapist.

The furrows across his brow deepened as the horses began to move. “Could they not find any smaller horses for this?”

She sidled next to him as he leaned against the ring’s wooden fence. “She’ll be fine.”

Grace and her roan colored mare plus three more riders and mounts made a slow pace around the ring. A guide flanked each child as the horses ambled around the circle. Other than the muffled sounds of hoofs plodding against sawdust, quiet prevailed in the outdoor arena.

Some of his tension eased as the horses made several uneventful laps around the ring. Grant leaned over. “She really likes this.”

Abby studied Grace’s impassive expression. “How can you tell?”

“She was playing in her room this morning while I was getting us ready. She caught sight of her helmet and boots as I was putting them in her backpack. That was it. Her favorite stuffed dog, Bobo, hit the floor and she tore off towards the back door. I thought she might be riding in her pajamas today. I like to have never got her back upstairs so I could dress her.”

Abby chuckled. “That’s good.”

Action in the ring claimed her attention as the guides began accelerating the horses’ pace to a brisk walk. Grace, still holding tight to the horn, bounced rhythmically in the saddle.

Grant gripped Abby’s arm. “I’m dying to duck-tape her to the saddle. Do those guides know what they’re doing?” He squeezed her harder.

Abby patted his hand and tried not to smile. “The

stables have the right credentials and all the handlers are properly trained."

"Are you laughing at me?"

"No." She blushed because she was a little amused by his white-knuckle parenting style. "I'm just surprised at how nervous you are. I didn't think anything frightened Captain Daredevil."

He winked then leaned in. "I have a confession to make. I'm a big scaredy-cat when it comes to my girl. Last week, Heather ended up sending me to the car."

God, if she already wasn't in love with him, that last statement would have done it. Gorgeous, fearless, dominant, his godlike perfection drew her like iron to a magnet, but it was his Achilles heel that bound her to him.

His attention suddenly jerked back to the ring. He raked his hands through his hair. "Are they galloping?"

Easing her arm around her Achilles. "Sweetheart, they're not. I don't even think that could be considered a trot." Abby steered him towards a picnic table she'd noticed on their way in. "Why don't we come over here. No one says you have to watch."

"It's probably a good idea." He shot a glance over his shoulder and let out a breath. "Thank goodness, I'm not going to have to face her dating. I'd probably have an aneurism."

"She might, you know." His worried gaze shot to hers. "I just meant, there's no knowing what things will be like in the future."

Man, I'm making matters worse instead of better.

"I know." He toyed with the edge of the picnic table. "That's what worries me. Who's going to watch over her when her mother and I are gone?"

Instinct told her he wasn't looking for a list of names of people who'd gladly look after Grace. She laced her fingers with his and leaned into him. All day he'd been uncharacteristically solemn, a perplexing change from his usual exuberance. She rubbed circles into the back of his hand. At least her attempts at distraction seemed to be working.

Finally, he broke the silence. "Did you just want the one child or would you have had more if you'd had the chance?"

Her eyes widened at his change of tack. "I don't know. I like kids so probably."

"I hate Grace is an only child." He shook his head. "Even though Katie is a lot younger than me, we've always been close. I just think it's nice to have a sibling."

Abby nodded. "Sarah and I aren't close, but she's the only person in the world who knows what it was like to grow up with our parents."

"Yeah." His voice sounded far away. "I don't think Katie remembers much about our old man, which is a good thing. But she's really good with our mom."

"Sarah and I had each other when our parents passed. That meant a lot."

Several heartbeats of silence passed while he continued to turn the table into toothpicks. "If the circumstances were right." His eyes locked on to hers. "Would you want to have another child?"

Her chest tightened, remembering her tender moments with Grace. With the stresses of raising a child on her own, her memories of Jackson's childhood, though sweet, were colored with worry. She couldn't imagine how lovely it would have been just to absorb the joys of motherhood.

For a split second, she considered giving an ambivalent answer, but he deserved the truth. She shook her head. "I don't want more children." Her biological clock played only a small role. She'd heard of a few women who'd had healthy children after forty-five. "I like where my life is headed, and I wouldn't want to start over again with diapers and midnight feedings."

A pained looked crossed his face. "I can understand that."

I failed that test.

She'd have given anything to have given him the answer he wanted. Several heartbeats of silence past. "What you say we take Grace to the park after this?"

"That would be great." His left-field question still claimed her attention. Their relationship was so new. The step from getting-to-know-you-fun to babytalk seemed like a giant leap.

"Afterward we can head to the house for dinner."

The present. The next activity. The pleasure at hand. That was as far into the future as they ever got. They also never talked about the elephant in the room, the one draped in the Union Jack. Beyond deciding they were exclusive, they'd never talked about commitment. She couldn't bring herself to do it now, even as her move to London loomed.

Tears stung her eyes, which was completely ridiculous considering until this moment she didn't think she'd ever been this happy with her life. Jackson was grown, married, and doing well. Financially, she was a secure as she'd ever been. Most of all, she was blessed to have a man in her life who was good to her and for her.

Abby blinked away the tears. “Sounds like a plan.” Tendrils of worry snaked through her, like anxiety kudzu intent on choking her happiness.

Chapter Sixteen

The next Saturday morning dawned with a sky as blue as a robin's egg. With mother nature calling her name, Abby let her inner farm girl have full rein. Lawn clean up, weeding, then plucking the best of her spring blooms for her contribution to the Davis family's Easter celebration later that day.

She'd just shucked off her boots when Grant's ringtone had her snatching her phone from her back pocket. "Hey babe, what's got you up this early?"

His low rumbling laugh set her blood racing. "Missing you. Would you like to come over today?"

More than anything. Which was why she needed to say "no." Spending every waking minute together would only make the move harder. "I do, but I wanted to finish off the bedroom today." She also wanted to ask if he'd visit her in London. The prospect of sounding needy kept her from voicing her desire almost as much as the fear he'd say no.

"I forgot." Disappointment laced his words. "I guess I should let you get to work."

"I'll see you tonight at your mother's." Expecting him to invest so much time on her when he had so many other obligations bordered on narcissism. He had enough of that type in his life already.

"Can't wait. Maybe we can slip back to the butler's pantry."

Nothing kept him down for long. Not even her emotional issues. "Sure. Your mother won't notice when twenty percent of her guests disappear." Her need to feel his body next to hers tested her resolve to keep her distance. She amended her I've-got-things-to-do statement. "If you want, I can come to your place tomorrow."

She could practically hear his smile. "Awesome and I can't wait to see you in a few hours. Even if I'll have to keep my hands to myself."

After hitting the end button, Abby stuck the flowers in a vase and moved down the hall to Jackson's old room. Three or four hours putting on the final touches and the place would be perfect. The butterfly print drapes and matching window cushions added just the right amount of whimsy. She'd also pulled some books down from the attic, thinking Ms. Griffin's girls would enjoy them. A dozen or so boxes of children's books lined the walls of the freshly painted room.

Several hours later, Abby had filled all the shelves she could reach without a ladder. "Darn it." She'd taken her folding ladder to school so she could hang her students' artwork from the ceiling. "I guess a chair will have to do."

Dashing to the kitchen, she snagged a chair from the set she'd bought in a yard sale several years ago. In an hour she'd need to change for the dinner.

Abby jiggled it to check for sturdiness. It seemed like it could hold her weight. With a stack of books under her arm, she pulled the chair towards the shelves and mounted it. No issues during the first couple trips up and down her improvised ladder.

A creak. A twist of the chair. A loud snap.

Every bone in her body felt rattled. Even her teeth hurt where her jaw had contacted the hard, wooden floor. Thankfully, unlike the elderly woman in the commercial for emergency pendants, she could move. Abby eased to her knees and after a few deep breaths to keep down her last meal, she inventoried her injuries.

She brushed her fingers over the goose egg already forming on her forehead. Since it was only tender and her head was no longer swimming, she probably hadn't given herself a concussion. Her wrist throbbed with every heartbeat. She gingerly pressed a finger on the bruise that was already blooming.

"Son-of-a-biscuit-eater." One touch told her it was broken. When she'd been hoping for an excuse not to attend Katherine's Easter dinner, this was *so* not what she had in mind.

She pulled herself to her feet using the remains of the kitchen chair. "Look at the chaos I've made." On her way down she'd pulled the drapes from the window, the chair leg lay splintered across the wooden floor, and books were scattered around the room.

She rolled her eyes at the mess and made her way to the kitchen. Then she snagged a bag of frozen peas and a clean dish towel on the way to the table. After a couple of minutes of deep breaths and mumbled curses, she reached across the table for her phone and pulled up Chris's number.

Shoot! He's in Charleston.

She moved her finger down the list of favorites and pushed Jackson's. It rang five times then went to voicemail. Next, she texted. *Your mom's done something stupid and I need you to come to the house.* She added a couple winking emojis, not wanting to scare him. While she waited, she peeked underneath the bag of peas. "Holy cow!" The bruising had spread and her wrist had swollen to twice its normal size. Next, she texted Katie with no response. "She's probably helping her mom with the party." Abby cast a glance around her tidy but empty kitchen. Hurt. In need of help. Alone.

Is this my future? My glorious second act?

Abby willed the tears forming at the corners of her eyes into submission. She'd managed to take care of herself for all these years. Today was no different.

It took ages for her to limp to her bedroom for shoes and her purse. By the time she made her way to the garage, perspiration had soaked her shirt. Defeat weighed on her. What choice did she have? It wasn't like she could wait and hope her wrist healed itself. She opened the door to the car and saw her next hurdle. The stick shift. She'd never be able to manage to drive Grant's car one-handed.

She slumped on the doorstep and stared at the pearl-colored beauty. Grant had been so concerned about her safety. Cared about her happiness. Had offered only support.

I should have called him first.

Shaking her head at her own stubbornness, she tapped in his number and prayed he'd pick up.

One ring. "Where've you been beautiful?" Inuendo laced his voice. He chuckled low and even with the throbbing pain in her wrist her body reacted to his words. "I know you weren't exactly looking forward to spending time with my mother, but I sure was looking forward to seeing you."

The image of him wrapping her in a tender embrace overwhelmed her. "I need you." The realization blended with the pain and doubled her over.

In a flip of a switch the sultriness evaporated, replaced with a demand. "What's wrong?"

"I'm hurt."

"Where are you?" Before she had a chance to answer, he barked again. "Dammit Abby, tell me where you are."

Her heart kicked into overdrive at his command, making her head swim. "Home."

"I'm on my way." The line went dead.

She'd barely had time to trade the soupy peas for frozen corn and to pop in a couple Tylenol before she heard the scream of his bike. He must have broken a land speed record getting from Johns Creek to her home in Decatur. The backdoor banged hard against the wall, causing Abby to jump.

His long legs chewed up the floor in a pair of strides and suddenly he was on her. His blue eyes crackled with tension as he looked her over. He hadn't said a word, the only sound being his deep breaths.

Abby shrank from him. She'd never seen him angry before. He leaned forward and brushed his lips over the knot on her head.

"I've aged a hundred years since you called me."

She eased her good arm around his neck and breathed in his dark, masculine scent. "Sorry." After a kiss on his cheek, she pulled back. "I'm pretty sure I've broken my wrist." She pulled back the bag of vegetables and held her arm up for his inspection.

Touching her as if she were made of spun glass, he gently ran his fingers over the bruise. As gentle as he was, a hiss escaped her lips. He brushed a kiss on her fingertips and then slowly guided her to the kitchen table. He shot her a look, leaving no doubt that he wouldn't put up with any of her nonsense. "Give me the keys to your car. I'm taking you to the hospital."

She didn't have the energy to raise a stink about to whom the car belonged and going to the hospital was a foregone conclusion. "They're right here." She slid them across the table. "I've just got to get my coat."

****

The only thing making the three hours sitting in the ER waiting room bearable was Grant's firm shoulder for her to lean on and his non-stop caresses.

He brushed her hair back from her face and planted a kiss on her temple. "I'm mad you didn't call me first," he growled low in her ear.

She took his hand, intertwining her fingers with his. His work-worn palms brought back delicious memories of the last time they'd been together. Lust bloomed in her belly, giving her a momentary break from the pain. When they were done here she had an idea for how to help him forget his anger. "Sorry." She leaned into his shoulder.

He chuckled. "It's okay. At least you finally came to your senses."

She had. Grant Davis was someone she wanted in her life, in whatever shape, form, or fashion they could work out. The Atlantic Ocean wasn't big enough to keep them apart if he was willing to make the crossing. Her independent streak wasn't going to be a limiting factor either. She buried her face as deeply into his chest as she dared with thirty-odd people nearby. "I wish the bones in my arm were as hard as my head."

Grant snorted a laugh loud enough to draw the stares of several people. Ignoring their audience, he cupped her chin. "I love how you make me laugh." His blue eyes snapped with excitement.

Abby's heart clenched. It was the first time either of them had used the L word. Did that mean he loved her? She certainly was falling in love with him. So hard it scared her.

"Abby Roberts."

She welcomed the interruption. The ER wasn't the location she'd envisioned when she finally worked up the courage to let those three words leave her lips. Grabbing Grant's hand, she followed the nurse back to an examination room.

Two hours, a wrist X-ray and a CAT-scan later, Abby was crawling the walls. After the initial examination, they'd given her something for the pain, but hours later, it had worn off. "How was your week with Grace?"

He brushed back a lock of her hair, tucking it behind her ear. "Don't feel like you have to talk. I know you're hurting."

She shook her head. "I want to. It keeps my mind off the pain." Her throbbing wrist wasn't the only thing on her mind. Though she'd come to the realization she wanted to continue seeing him after she left for London, Abby needed a distraction from all the other obstacles they still had to face.

"Are you sure?" He brushed a hand through her hair. When she nodded, he continued. "We had a great time, just the two of us hanging out. Her vocabulary is growing."

"That's good."

He offered her a tender smile. "It is, but I can't help wishing things were different."

More than anything she wished she could ease his worry. While giving him another child might alleviate one of his concerns, she wasn't in the place to make that offer. Still, she couldn't prevent the tide of regret washing over her. Abby turned her head so he couldn't see her swipe at her tears.

One thing she didn't regret was keeping the "I love you" to herself. Fortunately, before Grant noticed her tears an orderly came to take her to the Cast Room. Abby leaned her head back on the bed and closed her eyes as he wheeled her into the hall. There was a big gap between realizing how much she loved Grant and making the leap to telling him.

****

What felt like an eternity later, the glass door to the ER cubical slid open, jerking Grant to attention. He dug his fists in his eyes to roust himself as the nurse wheeled Abby into the room. "They gave her a sedative to set the bone, so she'll be groggy for a while."

As if to prove the woman wrong, Abby perked up. "When can I go home?" Her words slurred.

The nurse locked the wheelchair in place and helped Abby back onto the gurney. "It will be a little while, Ms. Roberts. I can't let you leave until you're more awake."

"I'm good. Tell Jason Willoughby he gets an A from Ms. Roberts." She eyed Grant with a lopsided grin. "Of all the orthopedic doctors in Atlanta, I had to get a former student."

A grin played at the nurse's lips. "I'll be sure to tell the doctor." Then she turned to Grant. "Is there someone who can stay with your friend when she gets home? She doesn't have a concussion, but she's going to be pretty sore for a few days."

"She's my girlfriend. I'll be looking after her."

Whether she wants me to or not.

Grant pulled up the thin blanket then pressed a kiss to her forehead. "Lay back and rest. The medicine will wear off faster if you don't fight it."

Abby shook her head but halfway in her attempt to sit up she slumped back and was out. Grant clutched her good hand. "Stubborn woman." He took in every inch of her while she slept. How had this force of nature tilted his world off its axis? In three months, his life had gone from barebones to a beautiful, complicated mess. Leaning over the bedrail, he pressed a kiss lightly on her lips. "I love you, beautiful."

Her eyes fluttered for a moment then stilled. *Thank goodness.* As much as he wanted to tell her, his gut told him she wasn't ready to hear it.

After God only knows how long Abby stirred. "Grant."

"I'm here, baby. Are you in pain?"

"Just groggy. I don't do pain meds well. Please tell me I haven't been giving the staff a hard time."

He couldn't resist. "No more than usual."

Abby covered her face with her cast arm. "Please take me home."

Grant pushed the nurses' call button. "I'm all over it, babe."

It took another couple hours but finally he eased the sedan onto her driveway and killed the engine. "Wake up sleepyhead." Scooting around the front of the car, he snagged the door just as she unfastened the seatbelt. "Let me get that, will you?" Just once he wished she'd let him take care of her without a fight.

He reached across her body, unlatched the belt, and before she could wiggle her way out of the deep leather seat he scooped her into his arms.

"It's my wrist that's broken, not my legs."

"Humor me." He carried her through the house. When they reached her room, his eyes shot to her bed. God, their love making had been sweet. Sensing how she guarded her privacy, her trust had bowled him over. As he'd promised from the first, he'd take things at her pace. As much as it killed him to leave, he had to.

Grant thumbed towards the bathroom. "Do you need some help getting ready for bed?"

A beautiful blush bloomed on her cheeks. "I've got it."

He pointed to the bathroom. "I'll wait while you brush your teeth and whatever else you need to do."

"I won't be but a minute." She hurried across the hardwood floor.

Grant ran through his game plan while he waited. There was no way in hell he was leaving her tonight, even if he slept in the chair in her room. He'd been toying with the idea of stripping down to his boxers and crawling into her bed when the bathroom door opened.

The bright pink cast did nothing to take away from her sex appeal. Wearing the same tank top and sleep pants he'd seen the day they'd gone out on his bike, she quickly slipped beneath the covers. After propping her arm up on one of the many pillows that decorated her bed, she turned to him. "I think I'm all set for the night."

Grant ignored the dismissal. "Not a chance." He toed off his shoes and eased himself down onto her bed.

"I'm not leaving you tonight."

She sank deeper into the bed. "Suit yourself. I'm too tired to fight." The comment held little weight since he caught a glimpse of a smile playing at the corners of her mouth. Keeping the pillow under her arm, she rolled over on her side. The fire in her whisky-colored eyes had softened. "Take your clothes off and get under the covers."

He didn't have to be told twice. With a kiss on the tip of her nose, he turned out the light. When he imagined the first night in her bed, he hadn't planned on a pink cast getting in their way and her loopy from pain meds. Since when did any of his plans with her work the way he wanted? Tomorrow was probably going to be no different.

Chapter Seventeen

Abby woke drenched in perspiration.

Darn hot flashes.

She scissored her legs to kick off the covers, but something heavier than the comforter had her hemmed in. *Oh!* As the heat from Grant's body burned through the remains of sleep and medication, her memories of the night before resurfaced.

This was a first for her. Any sleepovers had taken place at the man's home. She rolled to her side, careful not to bump him with her cast. Sleep erased the hard lines, making him look younger than his forty years. She traced her finger lightly over his cheeks and down to the cleft in his chin. How had she managed to wind up with such a hottie?

She glanced at the clock. While it was past time to let Grant know how she felt about him, it was still too early to call Jackson and Katie. After she took care of one more thing, she'd call them. Over muffins and coffee, she and Grant would simply explain their relationship. While she didn't have a crystal ball, she felt good about where she and Grant were. Surely Jackson and Katie would be happy for them.

She leaned over to run her tongue along his whiskered jaw. "Good morning, Prince Charming." He moaned and snuggled closer. "I see you're a morning person."

This time he pulled her into him hard, grabbing her cast as he did. "Oh, crap, Abby. I'm sorry." Rolling over to the bedside table, he snapped on the light and turned back to her. His eyes were wide as he looked her over.

"Did I hurt you?"

She ran her hand along the hard plane of his chest. "Relax. I'm fine. Remember I told you I was tougher than I look."

"Are you sure?"

Abby trailed her hand down his chest. "I'm more than sure."

"Good God, woman. I love you."

She jerked her head up, expecting to find a smartass grin on his face. Nothing doing. His blue eyes burned with lust. And love.

More than anything she wanted to shoot those three words back at him, but even as she opened her mouth to give it a shot, they caught in her throat. What if he decided he wanted children more than he wanted her? What if he didn't want the trouble of a long-distance relationship? Where would that leave her if she opened herself up and got hurt instead of happiness for her risk?

He touched a finger to her lips. "It's okay if you're not ready." In a motion too swift for her to track, he had her underneath him.

Afterwards, she breathed deeply, taking in his warm spicy scent as she came back into her body. Her fingers moved over his neck and shoulders.

"Sorry, I must be crushing you." He rolled off her, leaving her feeling bereft without the weight of him against and in her.

She settled herself over him, getting as much skin-to-skin contact as she could. Beginning with her face nestled in the crook of his neck and ending with her legs splitting his.

His fingers combed through her hair then roamed down her back, pushing down the sheet and blanket as he did. After a few moments of sweet contact with the rough hands she loved so much, his caresses grew lighter and slower. Abby let herself drift into rest, knowing she was ready to tell everyone she'd found the May to her December. She chuckled to herself. Okay maybe she was September, October at the latest.

Sometime later, Abby jolted awake at the sound of dishes hitting the floor.

"What the…" a familiar male voice growled.

Her son's voice had her rolling off Grant and pulling the sheets over their bare bodies. A blush bloomed on her cheeks as she took in Jackson's dazed expression. "Grant told you he was taking care of me."

His jaw muscles flexed. "He did. But he failed to tell me exactly what that care would entail." He took several breaths, his nostrils flared. "Mom, have you lost all sense of propriety?"

"Let me explain."

"Please don't try and tell me this isn't what it looks like. I'm not a child." His fist clenched as he spoke.

Grant snarled. "Could have fooled me. Sure, acting like one."

Abby pressed her hand against Grant's chest to keep him from having a go at her son. "Let me handle this." Tucking the comforter firmly around her, she gestured to the door with her casted arm. "I'll talk to you in the kitchen."

The slammed door echoed around the room. This was *so* not how she'd planned for Jackson to find out. She stumbled to the dresser for her clothes, then turned to find Grant pulling on his pants.

"Stay." She buried her face in his still bare chest. "I think this is something I should do on my own."

He pegged her with a stare, his eyes darkening to midnight. "I'm not going to stand by while he talks to you like that." His grip tightened around her arms. "Right now, I'd like to shove my boot up his ass."

Even if she didn't need it, she appreciated him coming to her defense. "Which is precisely why you should stay in here. I know how to handle my son."

"Alright, but I don't like this one bit." He took her chin between his thumb and finger. "If he pulls any more crap, I'm coming in there."

Abby rolled her eyes. No doubt he would. "I didn't take his nonsense when he was little and I'm not going to start now." She stood on tiptoe to kiss his cheek. "Give me a minute. Have a shower then I'll come get you. I'm sure we can talk this out like the rational adults we all are."

Jackson had his back to her when Abby entered the kitchen. At the sound of her footfalls against the tile, he jerked to face her. His glare showed the few minutes it had taken her to dress had done nothing to improve his frame of mind. Not since his early teens, when he'd been all hot temper and bad attitude, had she been on the receiving end of such a lethal stare.

Abby snorted. Fine with her because she was pretty pissed with him too. She planted her fists on her hips and dove in. "Since when was it okay for you to talk to me like that?"

He thrust his jaw out in defiance. "Since when did you become a cougar?"

"Wow, you certainly aren't holding anything back."

His eyes narrowed. "You raised me to speak my mind."

She'd also taught him how to treat women. Still, she did see things from his perspective. He'd never seen her even hold hands with a man much less find his mom in bed with one. Her mother's heart softened a little. "I know you're shocked, but I'm happy, so please be happy for me."

"I can't do it, and I won't be there to help you pick up the pieces when this all goes to ruin." He ran his fist through his hair. "For Christ's sake he's my brother-in-law."

The two of them had had several conversations about his desire to make a good impression on Katie's wealthy family. "I'm well aware of who Grant is."

"Are you also aware that he has a wife and child?" His words hissed through clenched teeth and cut her to the quick. He might not have ever seen her with a man, but he knew her history and for the two of them her past would never be fully put to rest.

She shut her eyes and prayed her voice came out calmer than she felt. "Ex-wife and yes, I've met them both. Grace is absolutely precious and Heather is charming and gracious."

Some of the heat evaporated from his expression but the set of his jaw and the hard lines around his eyes showed their confrontation wasn't quite over. He let out a slow breath then crossed the black and white tile floor to plunk down at the kitchen table.

Eager to set things straight, she did the same, resting her cast arm on the tabletop. Jackson reached across the table to take her hands. "I doubt Grant has told you everything. They may be divorced on paper, but he and Heather are very much a part of each other's lives."

Since she'd raised him on her own, he'd never seen parents sharing custody. Abby let out the breath she'd been holding. "That's to be expected. They have a child together."

Jackson shook his head. "There's more to it than that. You should have seen them yesterday at Mrs. Davis's house. They spent the whole time huddled together, talking, laughing and playing with Grace. Katie thinks Heather's still in love with Grant." He touched her arm, a trace of pity in his eyes. "Honestly, Mom, all the Davis clan expect them to reconcile. If they do where will that leave you?"

What did her darling son know of the real situation? Abby was certain of one thing: Grant would never say he loved her if he still had feelings for his ex-wife. She pegged him with her own glacial stare. "You're only saying that because you don't want me to make waves with your new family."

Bolting from the table, he hissed over one shoulder, "You're right. I don't. These people matter to me, so stop making a fool of yourself and embarrassing me." As the echo of the door slamming died, the sound of tires chewing up her gravel driveway filled the void.

Tired to the bone, Abby slumped down on her bed and waited for Grant to finish in the shower. The pain meds had worn off and her wrist hurt like a son-of-a-gun. She slipped under the covers, propping up her arm with a pillow.

When the water shut off, she braced herself for one more heavy conversation. How could she put voice to the questions wreaking havoc through her crowded brain? It wasn't like she could start with, "Why are you with me?" or "Do you know Heather's still in love with you?" Like there was a way for that to sound anything other than jealous, insecure, and bitchy.

The bathroom door opened, and he stepped out wearing a towel wrapped low on his hips and a scowl. He crossed the room in a pair of strides, his blue eyes the color of the ocean after a storm. "How'd it go?"

Why couldn't he crawl under the covers with her and the two of them forget the past half hour? "Not great."

"Tell me."

He meant well, but she'd heard enough harsh words for one day and repeating her conversation with Jackson wasn't going to change anything. She shook her head. "Later." Before he had time to argue with her, she propped up on her good arm and reached for the bottle of pain medication. "My arm hurts. Right now, I just want to sleep." Not that sleeping was going to make her problems go away, but she'd had all of this day she could take. She plastered on what she hoped was a convincing smile. "I'll call you when I wake up."

Grant brushed her hair back and pressed a kiss onto her temple. "I'm taking a house key. If I haven't heard from you by five o'clock, I'm coming back over."

The corners of her lips turn up. Those were not the words of a man only interested in getting her in bed. If only Jackson's concerns were off base.

While he lingered over her body in an embrace, she

ran her fingers through his wet hair. "It's a promise. I'll tell you then what Jackson had to say about finding his mom and brother-in-law in the throes of passion."

Vaguely, she heard him growl. Darn, that medicine was quick. "Yep," she slurred. "It was quite an eye opener."

Chapter Eighteen

A week after Abby's accident, Grant had come up with a plan to fix about a dozen of the issues he and Abby faced. All she needed to do was say, "yes." He tapped his razor against the edge of the sink as he rehearsed. "Abby, these past few months have been great."

That wasn't it. Sounded like the opening line to a breakup.

He rinsed the traces of shaving gel off his face and slapped on some aftershave. "Abby, I know I said I was content to take things at your pace." He shook his head.

For Christ's sake, if he led with that they'd never get to the part where he asked her not to take the job in London.

"Maybe I should start with the good stuff then work in the other part." He stepped into a pair of black boxer briefs then moved to the closet and unzipped the garment bag. "Abby, I love you and you'd make me the happiest man alive if you would consent to marry me."

After that he'd bust out the three-carat solitaire he'd stowed in his safe at work.

That's it! Short, sweet, and to the point.

Once he'd shown her how serious he was about the two of them building a life together, he'd tackle the Atlantic Ocean sized issue.

While he buttoned up his shirt, a HD picture of

how this would all work out played through his mind. Instead of staying in the gatehouse, he could move in with her. Then, if she still wanted a career change, she could run Help and Hope full-time.

After shoving his feet into a pair of loafers, he jumped into the new car he'd bought to replace the one he'd given Abby and headed to Davis Air Transport.

Operation Engagement was now in motion.

He hit the door to the hangar office and found his righthand-woman at her desk. "It's after seven. What are you still doing here?"

She leaned back from the desk top computer and stretched her arms over her head. "My ex took Matt and Lexi to Florida for spring break, so I thought I'd catch up on some paperwork." A wry smile crossed her face. "I could also ask you the same question."

"I left something in my office." He kept going. The last thing he wanted was to get cornered into answering Maggie's questions.

Ignoring the ton of paperwork on his desk, he pushed the chair forward so he could get at the small safe bolted to the floor. Lying on top of a nest of deeds, certificates and treasury bonds sat a small, black velvet box. He shoved it in his coat pocket and double-timed it out the door.

Then he thought of the nine hundred times a call from work had interrupted his time with Abby. "I have something kinda important to do tonight." His hand stole inside his coat pocket.

She pointed to the suit he'd worn for Katie's wedding. "Your outfit was a dead giveaway."

"Can you handle things here tonight?"

She nodded. "Unless the place catches fire, I won't

bother you."

"Excellent." He fisted the velvet box.

Then she folded her arms across her chest, a smirk plastered on her face. "Anything you want to tell me about?"

"Not yet." He wasn't a superstitious man, by why tempt fate. He sent her a backward wave. "Check ya later."

Grant unlocked the door just as his phone came alive on his hip. Hearing Maggie's ringtone stopped him with one foot inside the car. For a nanosecond he considered ignoring the call. *Dammit!* She wouldn't be hitting him up unless something had gotten critical in the two minutes since he'd seen her. "What happen?"

"Harry's fine." She stated the important part first. "There was weather in Birmingham and four-two-seven ran off the runway. The left strut got bent so the thing's not airworthy."

Thank God, it's no worse than that.

He checked the time. "Any chance you could take over the other legs?"

"I would, but I'm scheduled to take the Caribbean flights in the morning. If we switched that would put you out of the office through the weekend."

"That won't work." He had Grace beginning Thursday evening. "I'll be there in a second, and we'll start digging our way out of this dumpster fire."

An hour later, Grant swapped the monkey suit for his flight suit. Probably the only time in history he'd rather wear black and uptight than brown and comfortable. On the way out to the hangar he palmed his phone. "Hey there, beautiful. About dinner tonight, something's come up."

They planned to drive downtown where he'd booked a table at a nice restaurant. He could see her wearing a clingy dress that showed off her gorgeous curves. She'd have her hair pulled up, exposing the ivory skin of her neck.

"Okay."

They'd come so far since the first time he'd had to cancel on her. Still, her easy acceptance stabbed him.

"Sorry, sweetheart, one of the planes had a problem and I have to take care of it."

"Come over when you get done. I'll wait up."

Since breaking her arm, he'd spent every night in Abby's bed. It had been seven nights of bliss. His imagination had been on the mark, he fit perfectly in her space. She even had cleared a drawer in the bathroom for him.

"I wish it was as easy as that. I have to fly to Birmingham and from there I'm off to Jackson, Dallas, and then up to Little Rock. I won't be back until Wednesday."

"Then you're at Grace's the rest of the week…"

Between school, her work with Help and Hope, and his jam-packed schedule, God only knew when he'd get another chance to do this up right.

Like he was going to ask the woman to marry him over the phone. It felt like he'd been waiting a lifetime to get to this point and his anticipation needed a release. Maybe if he just got her mind to thinking over the situation she'd be ready to give him an answer when he got back. "I was hoping we could talk tonight."

Her laugh did sensual things to his body. Now why would we want to do that?"

"Most of the time I'd agree with you. I love when

we don't talk." Which was one of the reasons they hadn't discussed the future, the present was too good to mess with. *With the exception of Jackson, who still needed a boot up his backside.*

Grant scrubbed his palms over his cropped hair. "I want you to…" He was going to ask her not to go to London and was prepared to beg if he had to.

In the end he couldn't do it. He'd been trying to get her to take some chances since he met her. "The end of May is looking pretty big in our windscreen. I know I said we could take this at your pace…" His mind played over all kinds of commuter romance scenarios. Twelve months wasn't too long if he didn't think too hard about the days without hearing her voice and nights without feeling her body next to his.

"It means a lot to me, that you've been so understanding."

"I need to be looking in those gorgeous eyes of yours when I say this."

"Grant, you're really starting to freak me out. What's going on?"

"I want you to think about our options." If she decided to go, knowing she had a ring on her finger made it seem better. Not because he thought it would keep her from cheating, but because this way she could look down anytime she wanted and be reminded how much he loved her. "I want more of you." The words hung in the air between them. "I just want you to keep an open mind when we talk."

He wanted to drop those three little words on her. He loved her so much it made him mental but saying it would only make her feel pressured to say it back. As far as how she felt about him, he knew where he stood.

She loved him even though she had never used the words. He saw it in the way her eyes took him in.

"I can do that."

One of the mechanics caught Grant's eye, signaling the plane was ready. "Sweetheart, I gotta go."

"I'll miss you this week. Will you call me?"

She sounded okay, but she had a way of hiding her feelings behind a bunch of perfectly crafted words. He wished he'd thought to make a video call, at least that way he could read her better.

"Every night, promise."

Dammit, he wanted her to say yes.

****

"I can't leave you alone for a minute," Chris stated as he surveyed the damage Abby caused when she fell. Besides the books scattered across the floor, she'd also taken the curtains along for the ride on her trip to the floor. He stepped over the remains of her kitchen chair and unfolded his ladder.

She palmed a couple books with her good hand, passing them off to him. "It was more than a minute. You've been gone two weeks." The day after the fall, she'd come into the bedroom, looked at the disaster and considered calling FEMA.

In this case the F stood for "friend." He reached from his perch to take another handful. "I'm so sorry I wasn't here for you." Guilt shown on his sweet face.

"Don't be. Contrary to how it looks, I can take care of myself." She picked up a couple of the bigger pieces of chair.

She thought about the past week and the amount of time she'd spent rambling around her house. True, she was fine on her own, but it didn't mean she didn't miss her guys. In addition to Chris being up to his eyebrows in his antebellum remodel, Grant had been flying cross country for the past week. And Jackson… she wouldn't let herself dwell on the reasons why he wasn't around. Abby pulled her thoughts out of that tailspin. She and Jackson would patch things up. He just needed some time.

When she returned from disposing of the chair, Chris had rehung the curtains. "This room turned out cute."

"Thanks for helping me put it back together. Are you hungry? I've got some lasagna in the fridge I could heat up."

"I could eat." He folded the ladder and tucked it under his arm.

While Chris returned the ladder to his truck, Abby started dinner. Then in an easy, practiced way that spoke of the hundreds of times they'd done this, he set the table while she put a salad together. With all the changes in her life lately, Abby took comfort in the ritual.

"What's going on with the teacher exchange thing? You haven't chickened out, have you?"

"No." Her words came out a heck of a lot more certain than she really felt. She couldn't stand wishy-washy people, had never understood their indecision. Just weigh the pros and cons, make the choice with the most pros, and then stick to the decision. Easy, breezy. But lately she hadn't been so certain. Grant was too important to her not to have an impact on her decision. "Even if I wanted to, it's too late to back out. I've got Ms. Griffin to consider. If I don't go, there's no job and no house for her to come to."

Then the universe had gone and added a new kink to the situation. It was an enticing twist, but it upped the ante all the same. "Besides something new just came up. One of the other teachers contacted me about participating in a teacher exchange blog."

"Cool." He poured another glass of tea.

"There's more. The lady has published a couple nonfiction books on education, and she wants to see about turning our blogs into a book. She needs an answer from me by next week." Abby had written a couple articles for a parenting magazine and the chance to see her words in print again was a fabulous opportunity.

Why didn't her good news make her feel better? Some of her angst came from the fact she needed to be discussing this with someone else.

I can't wait until Grant gets back.

Maybe they could find some middle ground. After all, he did own a plane large enough to fly over the Atlantic. On the other hand, there were others besides the two of them in the relationship. Maybe she was asking too much of him. Wanting to curse the timing of the universe, she tried to envision a scenario where she could have both.

She'd always rolled her eyes at women who were dependent on a guy. Thought it was ridiculous to stake so much of their happiness on something as uncertain as a man. Well, the shoe was on the other foot now. When the person was as important as Grant had become, it was like trying to tie your shoes with one hand: doable but darn hard.

"Anyway, that's one more thing I need to decide about. Along with what personal items I can take."

Chris pushed his plate aside and stretched his long legs. "I can bring some of your things over. Don't forget I'm coming for a visit as soon as this house is finished."

"I haven't. Sometime in August, right."

"Yeah, jeez that seems like such a long way off."

"It does." She calculated how many weeks that was. Not counting the past few weeks when Chris had been working in Charleston, the two of them rarely spent more than a couple days apart.

"Don't worry. You're going to be so busy you won't have time to miss me."

"Yeah, I will." Her bestie wasn't the only one she'd miss. Without realizing what was happening, Grant had become an important part of her life. Although, she might be getting ahead of herself in assuming he would visit. He had a lot on his plate between work and his daughter. She didn't want to add another obligation.

Chris stood to clear the table. "Did anyone else say they were flying over?"

"My niece, Jessica, wants to come if Sarah will let her."

"What about Katie and Jackson?" His brow furrowed. "By the way, what's up with them blowing off our weekly dinner?"

She shrugged. "They're just busy." She tried to not think about not seeing the two of them for a whole year.

"They're still participating in the Help and Hope picnic tomorrow?"

"I'm not sure. I haven't heard from Jackson in a few days."

She needed to get off that train of thought.

Otherwise she was going to end up saying more than she needed to. "By the way, thanks for helping out. I know running a cotton candy machine wasn't how you planned to spend your Saturday."

Chris touched her cast. "Well, it's not as if you could do it one handed." He laughed. "But, if I'm going to be up by nine in the morning, I need to get my beauty rest." He planted a kiss in her hair before heading to the door.

"Sweet dreams." She locked the back door behind him. After that Abby puttered around the kitchen, her head too full to even consider getting her own beauty rest. Besides, she was hoping to hear from Grant. He'd kept his promise and called every night after he got Grace settled.

When the clock reached eleven-fifteen and he hadn't called, she figured he'd gotten sidetracked. She'd see him in the morning, Abby told herself as she went through her bedtime routine. The promise didn't do much for helping her wind down. Once she was tucked in, restlessness kept her plumping her pillow and tugging at the covers. Trying to distract herself, she checked her email then read. At midnight, she'd just turned off her e-reader when her phone went off. She made a grab for it, thankful no one was there to see how desperate she was to talk to him.

"Hey there, beautiful. I hope I didn't wake you."

"You didn't. How was your day?"

"Nothing worth talking about at work. Grace is good, just not wanting to go to sleep."

"I miss you. I was just getting used to you sleeping over, and now I have to readjust to having the bed all to myself."

A tiny fib lay buried in her admission. There'd been no getting used to having his six-foot, three-inch frame in her bed. From the first night it felt as if he'd always been there. With her cheek resting on his chest and a leg thrown over his, she'd slept deeply and woken full of energy.

"Tonight's the last night. I can come over after the picnic if you like."

The suggestive lilt in his voice heated everything below her navel. "I'd really like that." She imagined how good his weight would feel atop her as they made love. As much as she'd like to continue discussing what they'd do once they got in the privacy of her bedroom, she mentioned the main reason she hadn't been able to sleep. "Then we could have that conversation we've been putting off."

"Absolutely. I'm sorry about bailing on you."

He'd told her the same thing every conversation they had, and she'd answered in the same way each time. "It's not a problem. We both have obligations and we can't always do what we'd like."

"That's true, baby." Relief filled his words.

"Even though there's going to be people around all day, I can't wait to see you in the morning. It's been five days since I've gotten to hold you and I'm worried I'll forget how to do it."

"Until tomorrow then. Good night, beautiful."

Abby ended the call then turned out the light but didn't fall immediately asleep, despite feeling better having talked to Grant. After the picnic, when they were back here in her room, they'd work everything out. She rehearsed what she'd say to Grant. First, she was going to use those three words she should have said weeks ago. Then she was going to tell him that even though she'd thought about staying, she really wanted to go to London. She'd tell him about the book opportunity then after that she'd whip out her calendar and they'd mark off the days that he could visit. She'd repeat step one if he needed reassurance and sprinkle in some naughtiness if that was what it took to get the job done.

Despite the sweet conversation they'd had, doubt niggled at the back of her mind. Not that she was conflicted or confused because she knew exactly what she wanted: everything. She wanted Grant in her life, the new job in London, and her son's acceptance. Question was, could she have it all? The perfect second act.

Chapter Nineteen

"Ms. Roberts, where would you like us to set up?"

"Put the inflatable slide over there and the bouncy house between the ball fields and the lake." Abby pointed to a wide expanse of lawn.

The morning of Help and Hope's family day picnic had dawned clear and coming in the middle of dogwood winter was cold enough to make her glad for the sweater she'd grabbed on the way out the door.

She folded her arms around her middle and watched they guys unloading the truck. The board members and a couple of other volunteers were due at Magnolia Park within the next few minutes, but there was only one person who had Abby tuning her hearing for the sound of his arrival.

The distant roar of a motorcycle sent a spark of anticipation dancing up her spine. She listened as the high-pitched whine grew louder. Her imagination had his large frame leaning into the curves of Maxwell Road. He'd be at ease on the machine as he tested Newton's laws to the edge of good sense. And he'd look fine doing it.

He pulled in beside Abby's car then after killing the engine, tugged off the chrome helmet. Her imagination didn't do him justice. She could spend a lifetime trying to describe the snug way his T-shirt outlined the definition of his muscles and still not get it right. Abby tracked him as he stalked towards her, the sight of his stubble jaw sent chills skating across her skin.

She spared a glance over her shoulder at the delivery guys.

Disappointed to see one of them heading in her direction, she resigned herself that it would likely be hours before she could properly express how happy she was to see him. "Nice day for a ride." Her thoughts rewound to their private picnic a few weeks before. For her that day had been more of a turning point other than her first time on a motorcycle. Or making love outside. She'd welcomed a man into her bed. While to some it might not have been much of a hurdle, but for Abby it had seemed like a big step.

He shot her a look that made her skin go hot. "Everything get delivered like you wanted?" He was doing it again, using their need for discretion to drive her crazy.

He stood inches from her and the scent of his aftershave wafted towards her. She loved the way the sandalwood scent lingered. It took everything in her not to bury her face in his neck until this scent had tunneled into her brain. "Everything from Party Place was delivered, so I have almost everything I need."

He arched an eyebrow. "Almost? What do you still need?"

With practice, she'd gotten considerably better at playing this game with him, and his wicked grin let her know he enjoyed getting as good as he gave. She turned the legal pad for him to see. "I have a list we need to go over before the families get here. I'd like to run through it if you have a minute."

"Certainly." His gaze surveyed the open expanse of park. He pointed to a wooden gazebo at the far end of the park. Nestled in a small area with trees on three sides, it offered about the only chance they could enjoy a private moment. "I'll meet you at the gazebo in a few minutes. I'm sure we can check those items off your list." Then he ambled away.

Abby forced her mind to the task of checking off the inventory list of the things they'd ordered from the party supply store. The second the delivery guys set up the slides, she made a beeline for Grant. As she approached, his back was to her. Abby glanced around, surprised to find they were alone. She stole behind him and wrapped her arms around his waist.

"Quick, kiss me before someone interrupts us."

He twisted in her embrace, holding her at arms' length. His greedy stare raked over her body. "I've missed you."

At some point she should have gotten used to the way he greeted her. She hadn't and hoped she never would. Becoming bold under his hungry gaze, she did as she'd never dared before. She trailed her hand, the one not in the ridiculous hot pink cast, from her neck down to her hips. "You like what your see?"

"Very much." he leaned in and whispered. "I want you so bad, might have to steal you away later on,"

Desire fogged her brain, making it nearly impossible to think. "We can't. People might see." Abby buried her face in the crook of his neck and soaked in the warmth of his body. Her need to have him overwhelmed her. Even if all she could do was stand next to him, she was content with that. Like a riptide, the lingering dread she'd been fighting against tugged her. She felt like a leaf on the water buffeted by every wave until she wasn't sure which way to turn. What if the open mind he'd asked her to have meant he wanted her to reconsider going to London? If so, what would he do when she said no?

"You know there's a way of fixing it so we don't have to do this in secret."

Her mind shot to Jackson's face when she'd tried to explain her relationship with Grant. "Not now." Her gaze pleaded with him. She buried her face into the hard planes of his chest. "Right now, I just need this." Her words fell short of expressing how much she needed his arms around her.

"Whatever you want. Always." His fingers combed through her hair as he tilted her mouth up. He brought his mouth down hard against hers. His tongue plundered her mouth, turning their already heated kiss into something bordering on hunger. He groaned and pulled back, leaving her breathless.

"It feels like it's been weeks since I've seen you."

He stroked her hair letting his hand trail slowly down her shoulder and arm. "What are we going to do when stealing away gets a whole lot harder?"

"I don't know."

Why would the universe had presented me with a great job opportunity at the same time I found such a wonderful man?

At lease he sounded amiable to trying a long-distance relationship.

"What were the items on your list?" He continued with their teasing instead of pursuing the still unanswered question that lay between them.

She stood on her tiptoes and whispered several

naughty things that earned her a sensual growl.

"If I don't stop now, I'm going to have to take you into the woods." He pulled away. "I have an idea. Why don't you and Chris join Heather, Grace, and me for lunch?"

Abby shook her head. "Maybe next time. I don't think I could keep up the charade today."

A flicker of disappointment flashed across his face. "Tonight then. We'll make love, we'll talk, and then we'll make love some more. Tomorrow we'll lie around your place all day."

Abby grabbed hold to the promise, hoping he'd hear her out. "Yeah, I better go help set up the booths." She pulled out of his embrace.

He grasped her fingertips as she stepped from the shelter of the gazebo. "Before you go, I wanted to tell you again how much I appreciate you taking on this project. You amaze me with your capacity to love…" His eyes softened to the color of warm denim, turning her insides equally soft with their tenderness. "And I'm grateful you've given so much of that to me."

Her throat so choked with emotion, she had to cough a couple times before she could speak. "Tonight."

An hour after leaving Grant, family day was in full swing. The volunteers set up and manned the game and refreshment booths, leaving Abby with only a few organizational duties to handle. She waved to Chris who was up to his elbows in pink cotton candy then made a circle around the perimeter of the park towards the playscape. "Are you guys having fun?" She approached one of the parents from her school.

"Ms. Roberts," the young mom exclaimed turning

from the two boys she was watching. "Justin has missed you. When are you coming back to school?" She gave Abby a hug.

"I've missed him, too." She glanced at the six-year-old as he came down the slide. "I'm cleared to come back to work on Monday."

"Good to hear. I was hoping I could talk to you about a couple things next week."

"Shoot me an email in the morning." Abby hoped all was well. As difficult as her two-week absence had been on her, it hadn't been easy on her students, especially those who needed a routine. Before Abby could ask how Justin had been in her absence, his older brother interrupted.

"Mom, I'm bored. This playscape is for babies. You promised I could go to the bouncy house."

The woman's eyes darted between her two boys.

"Will, give Justin a little while longer."

Abby didn't know how single moms with more than one kid managed to divide their attention fairly. Grant referred to the technique he and Heather employed as, tag-team-parenting, which made the one she'd used with Jackson, man-on-man. What did parents do when the kids outnumbered the parents, especially when one of them came with a host of special needs? "I can stay with Justin."

"I can't ask you to do that."

Abby's gaze darted to Will whose dramatic pleading made her smile. "I'm glad to do it."

While Justin made laps up and down the slide, Abby pulled up the notepad app on her phone. She'd been jotting down ideas for potential blog topics and thought the challenges faced by single parents of kids with special needs would be a good one. She hoped her time in London would make her a better teacher, and so she added that to the list of reasons she'd use when she talked to Grant. *Jeez,* no wonder he'd once called her out for being too logical. She approached their talk of the future, like it was a debate to win instead of a matter of the heart.

With the sun almost directly overhead, the sweater that hadn't been quite enough was now too warm. After tugging her arm from one sleeve, she tackled the one stretched tight over her cast.

"Let me help you with that."

Her heart skipping a beat, Abby turned to Katie, holding out the arm she was struggling to free from the sweater. "Thanks, I'll be glad when this thing comes off."

Since the morning Jackson had walked in on her and Grant, Abby had reached out to her son several times. He hadn't answered, letting the calls go to voice mail. The fact, he'd had Katie return the calls minutes later, gave Abby hope she and Jackson would eventually work things out.

While Katie worked the sweater down an inch at a time, Abby wondered what, if anything, Jackson has shared with his wife.

"There you go." Katie handed Abby the sweater. A few tears shimmered in the young woman's red-rimmed eyes.

"Is everything all right?" Like her brother, not much got Katie down.

"Sure." She dabbed the corners of her eyes. "I'm just overly tired."

Abby led them to a bench where she could keep an

eye on Justin. "Let's come over here and talk. Tell me what's going on."

Katie thumbed away her tears. "It's nothing."

Being a mother-in-law should come with an instruction manual. If Katie were her daughter, Abby would feel freer to pry the problem out. But she wasn't, and she had a mother to confide in.

Likewise, if she were one of her fellow teachers or a friend, Abby would jokingly ask if Katie were having man problems. Considering the man in question was Jackson, that tactic didn't seem a good one either. In the end, Abby waited, letting her daughter-in-law dictate the conversation.

"Jackson and I had a fight this morning."

Abby waited a heartbeat, praying she'd say the right thing. "I'm sorry, sweetheart. All couples fight, even wonderful ones like you two."

"I know." Katie nodded. "It was over this family day thing. He said he needed to work on some cases, and I got mad and told him he'd been working too much."

Abby didn't believe that was the problem for a second. Guilt stabbed at her chest, knowing *she* was the reason for the couple's first fight. "Maybe he wanted to get it done so you guys could be together this evening."

Katie shook her head. "I don't think so. He's been acting weird for the past several weeks. Distracted, distant, it started right after Easter." She bit her lip. "I'm afraid he doesn't love me anymore."

"Katie, that's not it. I'm sure of it."

"How do you know?"

Abby clenched Katie's hand. "Because, he's crazy about you."

That answered the question of whether he'd told Katie.

She wondered what her daughter-in-law would think if she knew the reason for her husband's angst. Would she be happy for her brother or appalled at her mother-in-law's behavior? Either way Katie would know it wasn't her fault.

The explanation leapt to Abby's lips, but she bit it back. If Jackson had wanted to share this with his wife, he would have. "Why don't you head on home. I'm sure we can manage without you. You'll feel better when you've worked this out."

Katie threw her arms around Abby. "I don't know why mothers-in-law have such a bad reputation. You're the best."

"I hope you still think so twenty years down the road." Abby hugged her back. Then she watched Katie scoot across to the parking lot, adding another topic to the list she and Grant needed to discuss.

Chapter Twenty

Abby stared across the picnic area. Half a dozen families separated the spot Chris had chosen from the one where Grant sat with Heather and Grace. Those feet felt like miles, and her life which seemed on the verge of coalescing into a seamless fabric of perfection was unraveling.

Grant met her gaze and gave her a wink before turning his attention to his family. The sly gesture he offered Abby should have soothed her continuing unease. She watched them, guilt weighing on her for doing so and for wishing things were different.

"Do you need more lemonade?"

Chris's laugh pulled Abby from her thoughts. "I'm sorry. What did you say?"

"I. Asked. If you. Wanted. Some. Lemonade."

She nodded, letting him refill her glass.

Beneath his perfectly threaded eyebrows, his green eyes bored into her. "What's got you so distracted?"

"Just thinking about all the things I need to take care of." Hopefully her answer would pull him off the scent.

"Is that Grant's wife and little girl with him?" He followed her line of sight.

"Ex-wife."

How many times am I going to have to make that correction.

Then she made a point of turning her attention elsewhere. "Do you think I need to go buy more ice for the concession tent?" She chose a focal point one hundred-eighty degrees from where her mind lay.

"They have enough. Exes, you say. They look pretty cozy to me."

"I guess so." Jealousy was such an ugly emotion, still she couldn't quite get the green-eyed monster inside her tamped down. She couldn't bring herself to dislike Heather, much less hate her. She was an open woman who'd been lovely to Abby.

"I don't usually make judgments on other peoples' lives, but I gotta say whatever came between those two, they need to get past it. Anybody can see they belong together."

Her head jerked towards her friend. "What makes you say that?"

He gestured towards the happy trio. "Look at them. What a beautiful family."

Family! The word resonated in her ears. Regardless of what happened between Grant and her, those three would always be more.

"Look how well they get along," Chris continued, unaware how his words affected her. "I've seen relationships work on less than that."

The impact of Chris's words hit her full force. Her sister had said virtually the same thing. Abby finally saw what everyone else could, that Grant and Heather belonged together. She'd completely lost her mind thinking falling for Grant was a good idea. Problem was she had fallen for him, and who wouldn't. Despite her need to keep them under wraps, he'd accepted the relationship on her terms. What would happen when he woke up and realized the little she could give wasn't enough for him?

Grant said he only regretted things he hadn't done. What if he woke one day and realize what he should have done was reconcile with Heather, that he'd wasted his opportunity to give Grace a sibling?

Doing the right thing is going to kill me.

But do it, she would. It was for the best. If she removed herself from the equation, everyone would be the better for it.

All those days of worrying whether Grant would accept her decision to take the job in London had been for nothing. In the end, she took the option from him. She sent a silent thanks to the universe that she had the option of escaping for a year.

As if he could feel her emotions from twenty feet away, Grant's gaze shot to hers. His smile faded reading the stricken look on her face.

She cut her eyes towards the gazebo where they'd met this morning. She'd never make it until this evening to do this.

Grant's chin bobbed.

"Are you okay?" Chris touched her hand. "You're looking a little pale."

She cleared her throat. "I'm fine. I need to check on something. Can you take care of things here?"

"Sure." His brow furrowed. "I'll call you tomorrow."

Leaving him to clean up, Abby felt like a condemned criminal as she dragged her feet towards the gazebo. Her sins were many. As she approached the man she loved, she would add to them by hurting him.

It was the last thing on God's green earth she

wanted to do. Selfish Abby, the one who'd wanted something she had no right to, wanted it all. Acceptance from her family, an exciting career abroad, and for a man to accept whatever morsels of love she could offer. He deserved better. Better than she could give him.

Her words would hurt. Until more children filled his home, and he had a woman who deserved the kind of love Grant could give.

Following as soon as discreetly possible, Abby found Grant leaning against the gazebo's opening. Arms folded, long legs cocked, he was a titan at rest. Her pulse quickened both in response to his commanding presence and the awful task that lay ahead.

His hooded eyes tracked her movements as she walked towards him. Then, as she drew closer, he reached for her. He would have taken her in his arms, as he had that morning, always looking to sooth away her worries with his touch.

Every cell in her body screamed to accept what he'd always offered so freely. Instead, she put out her hand, her palm touching his chest. She fisted his shirt, knowing it was the last tender touch she'd have from him.

As he studied her, his brow furrowed. "What's wrong?"

His concern tore at her. From the beginning his thoughts had been for her. Abby had ignored what was right, even as those around her pointed out the truth. It was past time for her to fix that. "Me." Her throat grew tight with emotion. "I'm what's wrong."

"It can't be as bad as all that." He brushed a tendril of hair from her face. "Tell me what's going on, beautiful. I'm sure we can figure it out."

Tears welled in her eyes. There was no figuring this out, or talking it through, no compromises, explanations, or promises. There was simply what had to be done. If only she could find a way of doing the right thing without hurting him.

He'd fight her tooth and nail if she tried to explain he'd be better off without her. He'd also argue if she pointed out the number of people who'd benefit from her stepping aside. He'd only let her go if she used the one thing he'd never fight her on.

Only a lie would work.

Her stomach rolled at the thought. She hated lying, and she stunk at it to boot. It was a skill she was going to have to get good at to get through this.

She dove in, wanting the conversation over as quickly as possible. It was only a matter of time before she totally lost it and she'd never convince him if she were sobbing. "You know that conversation we've been putting off."

Grant took her by the arm, shaking his head. "Let's wait until we get back to your house. I want to hold you while we talk." He had them several steps from the gazebo before she could stop him from hauling her to the parking lot.

"No!" Getting lost in his embrace was part of the problem. He overwhelmed her good sense and had from their first touch. Abby jerked from his grasp. "I can't wait any longer." She drew in a deep breath, praying for strength. "I've decided I'm definitely taking the job in London."

Grant stopped then doubled back. He cupped her face, his blue eyes so tender they tested her resolve.

"That's fine, baby. Whatever makes you happy. We can work something out. I can come visit you as much as you like."

Abby cut off the visual her brain created. Wouldn't let herself imagine passionate reunions and stolen weekends spent exploring London. She'd known all along he'd be willing to do that. All her angst about whether he'd meet her halfway was misplaced, perhaps her heart's way of deflecting the issue.

Mastering the emotions fighting for release, she forced the lie to her lips. "Here's the thing. I don't want you to."

"Don't do this. Every time things get too real for you, you push me away."

The epiphany changed nothing. She made her voice cold, like she was speaking to a stranger rather than the man she loved. "I think it would be for the best if we didn't see each other anymore."

Confusion washed over him, as if she were speaking a foreign language. Then his jaw clenched. "Best for who?" His words came out as a roar. He circled her, raking his fingers through his hair before facing her. His heated gaze locked on to her. "Certainly not best for me."

"For me. This is what I need." She touched her palm to her chest. Abby threw herself into her act as if she could convince her heart as well as him. On some level she hoped it would be true, that giving him up now was better than being left down the road when he finally figured things out for himself.

"Did Jackson say something to you?"

Abby shook her head. "No." Which was part of the problem. Her son would rather anger and worry his wife than face a mother he was embarrassed by. She wouldn't further damage her relationship with her son, nor could she knowingly risk Jackson's place in his wife's family.

"I came to this decision on my own." She drew in a breath and pressed on despite the ache in her chest. "What we have…" She had to start thinking past tense. "What we *had* was lovely, and I'll never forget it. Let's face it. It was never going to turn into something permanent."

Grant paced as he barked back a response. "If this is about me saying I wanted more children. I was just thinking out loud." He took her by the shoulders. "All I want is you."

Still caught in his grasp, Abby raised her chin, forcing her gaze to his. Her heart stopped, knowing she'd been the one to put the hurt in his eyes. "I warned you from the beginning, I wasn't good at relationships." Like a killer going for the jugular, she finished him off. "It's not that I'm not good at them, I don't want one." Twisting the words he'd offered her, she drove the knife deeper. "You once told me you'd take whatever I could give." She opened her palms. "I've given you all there is."

Hurt flared in his eyes for a split second before he hid it behind an impassive mask. "I see." He released his grip on her. He hated her now. His clenched jaw told all she needed to know.

His hatred for her could fester for the next hundred years and it still wouldn't be as much as she despised herself. "Thank you, for understanding." She dug her fingernails into her palm to keep the emotions at bay. The movement shot pain through the mending bones in her wrist. She absorbed the stabbing sensation, feeling she deserved that and more for the pain she inflicted.

He drew in a breath, his eyes clenching in resolution. When he opened them, she had to look away from their iciness. She stepped towards the gazebo's entrance, unable to watch him leave. In fact, as his footfalls resounded against the ground she had to grab the bench she'd stumbled into to keep from following him. He stalked away and with every step, the cracks in her heart grew. Never had doing the right thing felt so wrong.

Chapter Twenty One

Abby rolled over in bed and caught a whiff of aftershave. She buried her nose good and deep in that sandalwood scent she loved so much. "Grant." She groaned his name, more asleep than awake. Her fingers tunneled beneath the covers, reaching for him. She found nothing but cold sheets, and the sudden deviation from her dream jolted her awake. "Oh, God." Tears formed again as the events of yesterday rushed back with sickening clarity.

For hours after Grant stalked away, she couldn't move from the gazebo. She didn't weep, though, far from it. Her fist muffling the sound, she screamed until her throat was raw. Abby raged against a fate that would have her fall in love only to require her to give him up.

Finally, her anger spent, she emerged from the protection of the gazebo. A couple families remained at the park, but thankfully they were absorbed with their own pursuits, and she was able to make it to the parking lot unnoticed. Abby had no recollection how she made it home. Her only thoughts behind the wheel were of finding some way of stopping the stabbing pain in her chest.

She stumbled through her house and collapsed fully clothed into her bed. The tears started then and hadn't stopped until her body couldn't make any more.

Silent sobs took over after that, until she finally fell asleep. It wasn't a restful slumber. Bent on torture, her unconscious mind replayed every touch, kiss, and word she'd shared with Grant.

Thank goodness there were some self-preservation impulses in her and they'd mercifully yanked her from her dream. The only point in reliving what she could no longer have was punishment for the pain she'd caused him, and she had the rest of her life to work out her penance.

Abby shifted in the bed. "Time to get up." She quickly found intent wasn't much help when her body wouldn't cooperate. She fell limp, but if she thought avoidance would fix things, once again she was sadly mistaken. With her face touching the sheets where Grant had lain next to her, her whole brain seemed one giant olfactory nerve. She pulled the cotton to her face and breathed deeply. Then she drew her shirt to her nose. She even sniffed her hair. His scent permeated everything.

Until last night she'd reveled in the way his scent marked her. Bolting out of bed, she then snatched the covers from the bed. Once she got started, she didn't stop until she cleaned everything that could be thrown in the washer or scrubbed with bleach.

Another very large, expensive reminder sat parked in her garage. How was she going to get that thing back to him? All day she'd half expected Grant to show up at her door. If he had there'd have been no way for her to keep up the pretense. She grabbed her phone to call for help.

Half an hour later, her back door opened. "Girl, I'm glad you called. I have got to tell you about my date last night." Chris's steps stalled. One look at her and his smile evaporated. "Good Lord, Abby, you look like death warmed over."

No amount of makeup could cover the effects of an eight-hour crying jag. He rushed to the table, touching her arm gently. "Is it your wrist?"

She wanted so badly to tell him 'yes' but now she needed her friend more than she needed her pride. "My wrist is fine."

He cocked his head. "What happened? I get the feeling I'm missing something here."

She took several deep breaths, trying to ease the tightness in her chest. "Grant Davis and I are..." Her voice broke. "He and I *were* having an affair."

Chris dropped into one of her kitchen chairs. "You were *what*?"

Abby clenched her jaw, angry not at Chris who had plenty of reason to be upset, but at herself for keeping the one person who might have talked some sense into her in the dark. She poured her frustration into her explanation. "An affair. You know dating, kissing, sex. That thing you've been after me to do." She waved her arms above her head like a lunatic as she rambled on. "Well, I've been doing it with my daughter-in-law's brother."

Her hysteria must have shown on her face since his indignation melted away. "Oh man, all those things I said yesterday. " He took her hands in his, asking her softly. "Why didn't you tell me?"

She struggled to recall her brilliant logic for keeping things on the down low. "I wanted to be discrete in case things didn't work out." As the words left her mouth, she realized a part of her always thought it was a matter of *when,* not *if* things went sour for them.

Chris shook his head. “How long has this been going on? Was it serious?” He waved his hand in her direction. “Of course, it was serious. I can look and see.”

“Yeah, I…” Abby’s words trailed off and it was several seconds before she could speak. “I love him.”

He blinked. “Did he break up with you?”

She shook her head. “No. I did.”

“Was it because of what I said?” Chris took her hands in his. “You know I don’t know my head from a whole in the ground.”

Abby waved her hand, cutting his concern off. “Not because of you. It just wasn’t right. I’m leaving for London soon, and I don’t want to try to manage a long-distance relationship.”

“But if he loves you.” Chris narrowed his eyes.

She should have known better than to attempt to fool him. “I broke it off because I love him…” She put her hand over her mouth to stop a sob that was threatening to escape her lips. After a second she tried again. “I love him, and I want what’s best for him. He needs to give his marriage to Heather another shot, and he’ll do that if I’m not in the picture.”

Chris wrapped an arm around her shoulder. “Baby girl, you deserve to be happy, too.”

She squeezed her eyes closed. “I will be, eventually.” Maybe if she said it enough it would come true. “I’ll go to London, have a good time, and forget all about Mr. Sex-on-legs.”

Enough of the pity party!

She stood. “First, I need to get the outrageously

expensive car he loaned me out of my garage."

"Don't even worry about it." He pulled out his phone. "I'll get a couple guys from my crew to swing by here on their way to Charleston." He cupped her cheek. "You know if you need me to stay here tonight, I can."

He'd already done so much for her over the course of their friendship. She wasn't going to let him jeopardize his business. She tried to make her voice sound light. "What, are you crazy? Only one of us can lose their mind at a time. Go, I'll be fine."

"Do you want me to call Jackson?"

"Heck no. He saw Grant and me together and flipped his lid. I'm not ready to hear an I-told-you-so from my kid."

"He. Did. What?"

The anger in his voice reaffirmed her decision. She'd already caused enough problems for this family, and she didn't want to turn a tear which could heal into a chasm. "It's not an issue anymore now that Grant and I are no longer together."

"I'm so sorry." His serious expression softened as he smiled. "He loves you, and I know he'd want to be here for you."

"I want to lick my wounds in private. Thank you very much." Abby drew in a breath. "Now, tell me about your date."

He chuffed and rolled his eyes. "Are you kidding? You don't want to hear about that train wreck. Let's write off relationships. We'll be two old maids together."

Love for him tightened her chest. Even his weak attempt at a joke made her smile. "That sounds like a plan. When we get too old to live by ourselves, we'll move in together. It'll make it easier for Katie and Jackson to look after us that way."

Chapter Twenty Two

Abby scanned the food-laden table. "Where do you want this?"

Chris took the bowl of chocolate biscuits with one hand while scooting a plate of meat pasties over with the other. "The guest of honor doesn't work at her own party."

"Just trying to be helpful." She scanned the room. "You know, if you decide you want to get out of the construction business, I think you've got a future in party planning."

He'd sweet-talked her into having a big farewell party, and in his usual attention to detail was throwing a British themed event. His living and dining rooms were swathed in an Anglophile's dream, with everything from cutouts of the royal family to Union Jack bunting and a cake shaped like Big Ben.

The Washington D.C. orientation began in two days. From there on to London. Abby let out a long, slow breath to calm the pounding in her chest. "Boy, this month has flown by." That was good on several levels, one of which was that it kept her mind off of Grant. Mostly. Sometimes.

She fingered the aquamarine bracelet he'd given her for her birthday. Sending back the over-priced car had been as easy as walking away from a hundred-pound box of chocolates. Sure, it was cool to have.

Really, who needed all that? Relegating the symbol of a happy period in her life to the bottom of her jewelry box, not so much. "I need something to do. Otherwise I'm going to take up cigarettes or nail biting."

He slipped an arm around her waist, giving her a gentle squeeze. "Nervous?" His green eyes danced. He'd been so excited about her new job, that she'd have thought it was he who was spending the year abroad.

She hugged him back, holding on hard for a few seconds. "A little." Not cold feet. The teacher exchange program represented an absolute godsend, a chance to heal. What was she going to do without Chris? And Jackson and Katie. She'd never been away from her family for more than a week. Much less three months until Chris came in August.

He hip-checked her on his way to the bar he'd set up on his buffet table. "Don't be. Everything will be fine."

Abby fiddled with the bracelet again, trying to keep her hands busy while her mind ran on an endless loop. There were still loose ends to tie up. "You'll be sure to send me my mail and check that the lawn maintenance company cuts the grass." Her mind raced in a hundred directions then zeroed in on the woman she was trading places with. "And you'll look in on Miss Griffin. I want her to feel at home here."

Chris handed her a pink gin concoction with a patient smile. "She's no replacement for you, but yeah, I'll check in with her." He made a shooing motion with his hands. "Now go. Sit. Enjoy your friends."

Abby wandered into the living room, stopping off to give first Katie a hug then check on Jackson. He looked up from the conversation he was having with his

Uncle Tripp and gave her a wink. Just as she'd hoped, things were back to normal between her and Jackson. She squeezed his shoulder and moved to her sister, Sarah.

"Would you like something to eat?" She took a seat on the sofa next to her. "There are soft drinks in the other room if you want one."

Sarah shook her head. "I'm fine. Katie fixed me a glass of tea." She smoothed her hand over her cherry-red skirt that she'd paired with a white blouse and royal-blue scarf.

A sisterly tribute to Abby's destination? At least Sarah was trying. Since she'd walked into Chris's house, she hadn't made one cutting remark or offered Abby one of her famous backhanded compliments. "Don't forget you have an open invitation to visit while I'm in London. There will be plenty of room in the flat."

Sarah pressed her lips together and shook her head. "That would be too far to go. Besides Tripp and I wouldn't know how to get around in a big city like London."

Abby wasn't going to press. Making the trip to Turks and Caicos for the wedding had been the adventure of a lifetime for them. "At least think about letting Jessica come over on one of her breaks from school. I promise not to let her get lost or swept off her feet by some rakish duke."

"We'll see."

Abby doubted her sister would lengthen the umbilical cord that far but at least the offer wasn't shot down. She started to get up but Sarah tugged on her hand.

Her grey eyes turned more serious than usual. “You always were the brave one in the family.” She reached over to tuck the strap of Abby’s bra under her sundress. “I wanted you to know I’m proud of you for taking this job.”

“Thanks.” The complement must have cost Sarah dearly. Their diametrically opposed lifestyles had been a large reason for their strained relationship. “That means a lot to me.” Abby patted her sister on the leg. “I need to mingle a little bit, but I’ll check back with you in a while.”

Abby made the rounds, speaking to all her guests and making similar offers to be hospitality central to all who wanted to come across the pond. She sidled up to Chris on her way out to the deck behind his house. “I’m going to get some air.”

He turned from talking with their neighbor from across the street. “Don’t disappear on me. I’m making toasts in a few minutes.”

“I won’t, just need a little break from being Popular Pattie.”

Abby circled the perimeter around Chris’s pool. Between making up with Jackson and her sister’s praise, she felt like all the loose ends were winding into a tidy ball. There was one thread that refused to join the others.

Hopefully in time Grant would forgive her.

****

“How many green blocks do you have?” He smiled when Grace held up five chubby fingers. Spending time with her provided his only solace these days. He rubbed his sternum. Four weeks and the sucker-punched pain lingered.

Heather walked into Grace's room and sat down at the low table where Grant and the three-year-old were putting together a block tower. They'd made the parental hand-off a little while ago, and she was in the process of heading out to her condo in the city. "Are you happy with the way things are?" Her body language screamed there was certainly something that *she* wasn't happy about.

His first thought had been *hell no!* But she wasn't referring to his love life. "Yeah. Why?"

Heather combed her fingers through Grace's hair. "You're not looking to make any changes to our relationship, are you?"

"Changes?" He folded his arms across his chest. "You know I'm no good at reading between the lines." If he was, he'd have understood what Abby really meant when she told him she didn't want to see him anymore.

"Did you buy an engagement ring?"

Grant clenched his eyes. After the breakup, he'd been in a fog for days. He barely remembered staggering into the kitchen downstairs and shoving the ring in a drawer. He let out his breath all at once. "Yes." Then he held up his hands to ward off the barrage of questions headed his way. "But not for you."

A smile played at the edges of her mouth as she made the keep going motion with her hands. When he didn't answer right away, she grumbled. "Talking to you is like pulling teeth. Who did you buy the ring for?"

"Abby Roberts."

Heather blinked several times. "I didn't know you two were dating."

"We're not."

She barked out a laugh. "She's going to be pretty surprised when you give her that ring."

Grant got to his feet and began pacing. This was not a conversation he wanted to have with anyone, least of all his ex-wife. "We were seeing each other, but she broke it off when she decided to take a teaching job in London."

She stared down at Grace's little table. "That's too bad. I'm sorry."

He didn't deserve Heather's sympathy. The mess was his fault. Perhaps if he hadn't pushed to make their relationship public, or mentioned babies, she wouldn't have felt cornered. "No big deal. Shi…." He shot a look towards Grace, minding his language. "Stuff happens."

"Why did she break up with you?"

Reliving what had happened with Abby wasn't high on his must-do list, but he couldn't help feeling he'd missed something. He pressed his hands to either side of his head. Maybe if he squeezed hard enough, his brain might pop out a clue. The morning of the Help and Hope picnic everything had seemed fine. She was more than glad to see him and they'd decided to meet back at her house later to discuss what to do about her new job. After that he'd spent the rest of the day with Heather and Grace. A thought niggled at the back of his mind. Abby had always seemed okay with the amount of time he and Heather spent together. She encouraged it even. "Holy…" He clamped his hand over his mouth before the rest of the phrase slid between his lips.

"Surely she didn't." he groaned. Heather's eyes widened. "What?"

"I'm not sure, but I think Abby thought if she

broke things off with me, you and I would get remarried."

"Nooooo." Heather plunked down on the end of Grace's bed. "What are you going to do about it?"

He shook his head. "Nothing. It's too late. She's leaving in the morning." Katie had been keeping him posted on Abby's agenda.

Heather narrowed her eyes. "Who are you and what have you done with my ex-husband? Because the Grant I know wouldn't have given up so easily."

Her mocking words were a verbal kick in the ass.

She's right.

Grant wasn't going to let Abby leave without hearing him out. If she truly didn't want him, that she wanted to start a new chapter of her life, he'd back off. He needed to make sure she was making that decision based on the truth: that the only woman he wanted to marry was her.

He bolted towards the door then just as quickly spun on his heels. "Can you cover for me?"

"Of course. Go, before she gets away." Heather joined Grace at her table. "Wait. You're forgetting something." She tossed the black velvet box to him. "Nothing says please hear me out like jewelry."

On the way out the door he punched up his sister's number. "Katie, where's Abby's farewell party?"

****

Abby jerked her attention to the sound of loud voices. Grant erupted from the house and stalked towards her. One look at his snug t-shirt and jeans and her body heated, knowing exactly how good the well-worn cotton and aged denim felt under her hand.

"Grant. I didn't know you'd been invited." She

went for light and casual as she spoke but failed miserably. A month had done nothing to lessen the pain of seeing him again.

Chris and Jackson followed quickly on Grant's heels, with her son cutting off Grant's trajectory. "He wasn't invited."

Grant towered over him, menace in his eyes. "I need to speak to your mother alone."

"Don't you think you've hurt her enough?" He pushed against Grant's chest when he tried to outflank him.

Abby hadn't provided her son with details of the breakup, just kept to the barest facts. Shame from the hurt she'd caused rushed out. "Grant has never done the first thing to hurt me. I broke things off."

Shock washed over Jackson's face. "Because of me?"

"Partly." I couldn't stand what our relationship was doing to you."

Jackson shifted his focus to her. "I've been so selfish." He took a breath. "I just want you to be happy, no matter what."

Emotion clogged her throat. "That's what I want for you as well." His sentiment helped but ultimately changed nothing. She turned to Grant. "I want you to be happy, too."

She searched his face, looking for signs of acceptance. Or anger. She'd certainly earned that. Abby found none, just the stubborn set of his jaw.

I've never given him the chance to say his piece.

"Can you guys give us a minute?" Neither made a move to leave until Abby shot Chris a pleading look.

"Come inside." He took Jackson by the arm. "Your

mom can handle this." After a scowl directed at Grant, Jackson return to the house.

Grant closed the distance between them, until his body became a wall that blocked everything else from view. He glared at her from underneath hooded eyes. "We need to straighten a couple things out."

Abby clenched her fist, bracing for the recriminations she deserved. "First please let me say this." Tears welled in her eyes. "I truly regret the way I handled things back at the gazebo." She also owed him the real reason she'd pushed him away. "However, I do think it's best for everyone if I go to London and you work things out with Heather."

Heat flared in his eyes. "Listen, if you don't want there to be anything between us, that's one thing." His voice softened as he continued. "But understand this. Heather and I are never getting back together." He stroked her cheek with the back of his hand. "How could you think I could remarry Heather when I'm in love with you?"

Abby opened and closed her mouth several times, trying to put her thoughts into words. "I don't see what attracts you to me." She flailed her arms around trying to make her point. "You could have someone younger, prettier, some woman who likes skydiving and scuba."

He pinned her arms by her side. "Don't you see from the moment you asked me to call you Abby instead of Ms. Roberts, you're the only one I've wanted." He bent down to brush a kiss over her lips. "The only one I could even think of." He feathered the kiss across her cheek. "You've got me so tied in knots, it's a wonder I can even function."

Even as he was doing exactly what she wanted him

to do and saying what she'd longed to hear again, fear screamed louder. Eventually, he was going to want someone who could love as openly as he. "I don't see how this can work out."

All the passion bled from his face. He thumbed the tears that trickled down her cheeks. "Oh, beautiful, always so cautious." He pressed a single kiss on her forehead. "Thanks for hearing me out." He let her go and turned towards the house.

How could Sarah ever think her brave? Going to London wasn't brave. It was the same job in a different location, a risk with training wheels. Bravery wasn't even telling Grant she loved him. If she truly were brave, she'd admit the way he loved her scared the ever-lovin' crap out of her. God, she wished she were different.

Frozen there by the pool, she studied his retreating form. "No more regrets." If she wanted to be different, she needed to act differently.

He turned. "What?" Pain contorted his handsome features.

Abby bit her lip. She'd been the instrument of that hurt. A hurt she could also heal. And remove the mistaken notion that she didn't love him. In a way he deserved to hear. "There are a couple things I regret leaving undone. I'd like to fix them if you'd let me." She took him by the hand, interlacing their fingers. "I told Chris I wanted to say a few words to my guests. Please come inside. I'd like you to hear my speech."

He bobbed his head and let her lead him into Chris's dining room. The guests huddled in the small space, with a glass in hand. She reached for two champagne flutes, passing one to Grant. The plan she and Chris had worked out was he would say a few words then she'd go afterward. Abby eyed her friend, signaling there'd been a change in plans.

Lord only knows what they'll think.

Only one opinion counted and that gave her confidence. "I never intended for things to turn out this way. It was just supposed to be one dance." She looked up at Grant. "But he talked me into one more. Then he kissed me." His face exploded into a grin.

"I tried to keep you away, didn't I?"

He nodded, then took her hand and began rubbing her knuckles with his thumb. Her pulse thrummed in her veins, and she needed to take several deep breaths before she could speak. "We even tried the cordial relations route, but eventually you wore me out."

He raised her hand to his lips, pressing a kiss into her palm. The quiet murmurings of her guests swelled. "Awww."

She made a point of looking at her family who were standing in front, wide eyed. Abby noted her sister's face was a contorted mess. Probably thinking only a spontaneous pole dance would be more horrific.

"Then I had to go and be my own worst enemy. All because I thought it was too risky. Goes to prove, just because you have a couple degrees and some age under your belt it doesn't mean you're smart."

She slid her arm around Grant until she was grafted onto him, could feel the heat of his body and breathe in his warm masculine scent once again. She didn't give the first-flying-fig what anyone thought of her PDA.

Abby tilted his face to meet those blue eyes. "Grant Davis, I love you." She punctuated her speech by dragging his mouth down to hers.

The crowd erupted into cheers, cat calls, and applause despite only a few of the guests having a clue what her drama bomb meant. Abby ignored them all, reveling in being exactly where she needed to be. After a moment when it became obvious she had no intentions of explaining herself or letting go of Grant, her audience left them.

He tilted her face to look at him. “I don’t want to keep you from going to London if that’s what you really want.”

Abby closed her eyes. Emotion welled. “Your support never fails to touch me.” She ran her fingers along his whisker shadowed jaw. “The adventure of living abroad pales compared to what life with you will be. I can’t wait for both.”

A devilish grin curled his sensuous lips. “If that’s the case.” He dropped to one knee then brought out a small box that he opened. “We can begin our adventure as husband and wife whenever you’re ready.”

“Yes, yes, yes. And *yes!*”

Once she’d finally broken through her wall of doubt, she wasn’t holding back. She threw herself into his arms, tears of joy streaming down her face. “And I know just where we need to have the wedding.”

Epilogue

One year later, Turks and Caicos

"I still can't do hair." Chris took a small cluster of flowers from Abby's trembling fingers.

In lieu of a veil, she'd chosen white orchids for her hair, which in her imagination would rest on the chignon at her nape. Thank goodness despite his insistence, her bestie was good with hair pins. She smiled at his reflection, "Some bridesmaid you turned out to be." She pointed to where she wanted the flowers.

In fact, he took his duties so seriously he hadn't left her side all day. He'd also escort her down the aisle to meet her groom. "Before Katie gets back with your bouquet, I want us to have one more of our talks." He fixed the flowers in place.

"Don't you make me cry. Between my bridal shower, Jackson's toast last night, and Heather's surprise wedding gift, I've been teary-eyed more in the last week than I have in the past decade."

Once the initial shock wore off, Grant and Abby's friends and most of their family had jumped at the chance to help them celebrate their marriage. Katie was delighted to have Abby doing double duty as both mother-in-law and sister-in-law. She'd only pouted for a second or two at being kept in the dark.

Katherine Davis had been another story altogether. She, along with Sarah, headed the unofficial Shocked and Appalled committee. The one person who so often got painted as the villain in these stories became Grant and Abby's champion. Thinking about Heather's efforts to have Grace at her father's wedding brought tears to Abby's eyes. She widened her gaze and fanned her face trying to keep the waterworks at bay.

Undeterred by Abby's pre-wedding emotions, Chris handed her a tissue. "You have on waterproof mascara, so hush and listen." He took her hands, his green eyes locking on to hers. "You don't have to go through with this. Just say the word and I'll have you out of here in a flash." He ran his assurances together in a one breath run-on sentence.

Abby's jaw went slack, but before she had time to voice her shock, his face split into a wide grin. "I know this is what you want. I just thought since I'm giving you away, I needed to act like the father of the bride."

She twined her arms around Chris's neck, grateful no matter what he had her back. "I'm so happy. Wild horses couldn't drag me away in case you're worried about the temperature of my feet." She pulled back, dabbing at tears which despite his jest were still pooling at the corners of her eyes. "Once Katie gets back with my flowers, I'll be ready to go."

Right on cue, Katie burst through the door. Her blond hair flying, she skidded to a halt. "Oh my goodness, you're gorgeous. Grant's going to have a fit when he sees you."

Abby brushed her hand over the knee-length ivory dress she and Katie picked out. With spaghetti straps, an open back, and a few sequins at the waist, she could easily have worn it to a summer cocktail party or the beach as was the case.

Still beaming, Katie handed Abby the bouquet of white orchids and roses. "I'm totally claiming credit for this romance." She winked. "Do you have everything?"

"Absolutely." Abby wasn't referring to the traditional old, new, borrowed, and blue her matron of honor, Katie, had seen to.

In her wildest imagination she could have never envisioned being the bride, and now that the impossible had come true she couldn't imagine wanting anything more.

"Then let's go. Jackson's only going to be able to keep Grant occupied for a little while longer. He's already threatening to come get you if you're late."

The words had no more left her lips when the sound of fist against wood echoed around the hotel suite. "Abby, open up. I need to talk to you."

Katie scurried to the door. "No, you don't. This isn't your first rodeo. You know good and well it's bad luck to see the bride before the wedding."

"I don't need to see her. I just want to talk." Stress had turned his normally sultry voice to thin and reedy.

Hearing the anxiety in her soon-to-be husband's voice calmed Abby's nerves. Grant hadn't appreciated one bit that he'd had to spend his last night as a single guy without her. Nor had he wanted to make himself scarce while Katie and Abby had enjoyed a spa day. He'd called every hour until Jackson had taken his cell phone away.

"All right, but just for a second." Abby moved through the plush carpeting in the outrageously overpriced heels Grant insisted she needed. After engaging the chain lock, she opened the door. "Sweetheart, I promise I'm not going to change my mind. I have no plans to be the runaway bride, no matter what Chris suggests."

"What?" He reached for her through the open door.

Abby clasped his searching hand, patting it like she would a child's. "He was just teasing. Now what did you need to tell me?"

"I wanted to give you your wedding present." Grant tugged her wrist.

Keeping the rest of her body hidden from view, she let him draw her arm through the door's opening. "You didn't have to give me a gift." He attached something cold and heavy to her wrist before pressing a kiss into her palm. Abby drew her arm inside to see a diamond tennis bracelet joining the aquamarine one she never took off. Her breath caught. "It's gorgeous."

Gracefully accepting his over the top gifts was a work in progress. His latest extravagance probably cost more than her first car, but sharing his wealth was how he showed people he loved them. "You realize if you keep this up, you're going to have a very spoiled wife on your hands."

"I'd like nothing better in the world." He reached for her again.

She was never truly going to be comfortable with his money, but the good thing was he totally got that about her. He hadn't pressed her to quit her teaching job, nor had he asked her to sell her home. A fresh wave of emotion expanded her heart even more than his love already had.

"Close your eyes and put your face up to the door." Once his handsome face appeared, eyes obediently clenched, she leaned in to press a kiss to his lips. "That's a little something to hold you over until the ceremony."

He moaned into her mouth. "That might just be enough." He then slipped back to his side of the door.

Abby closed the door and turned to her bridal party. "Let's get this show on the road."

Fifteen minutes later, she stood behind a pair of closed French doors trying not to strangle the bouquet in her hands. "You ready?" The music began.

Abby nodded and with her arm tucked into Chris's, followed Katie to the hotel's patio. Her gaze darted to their guest of honor, Grace, who sat quietly on her mother's lap. Then her devilishly handsome groom caught her attention.

Wearing a beige linen suit and a smile that lit up her insides, Grant stood between Jackson and the officiant.

"Dearly beloved," the justice of the peace began, sending her pulse into triple digits.

Abby's eyes never left Grant's as they repeated those binding words. With the vows complete, Grant pulled her into his arms. A grin flashed across his face seconds before he dipped her deep and kissed her long.

He finally let her up for air. "Mrs. Davis, would you care to dance?"

"Yes, thank you."

The five-piece band began the opening measures as he steered them to the poolside deck. Then the vocalist belted out the soulful lyrics, doing justice to jazz great Etta James about how it felt to have found her love.

"At last, indeed."

Their surroundings disappeared as she gave herself

over to the soulful lyrics and pounding surf, the scent of his aftershave, and the feel of her husband's arm. Going by the way Grant's hand had slipped to her bottom his mind had leapt ahead to the honeymoon.

Which was more than fine with her, but while her thoughts had joined his, when he made a quick and slightly awkward turn, she stumbled. "We are so not doing that again."

Abby glanced over his shoulder to see the pool inches from her shoe. "I agree. There are some aspects of that night which shouldn't be repeated."

They moved silently together for several measures, caught in their own little bubble. "Are you happy?"

Abby buried her face in the crook of his neck. "Unbelievably."

His laugh rumbled against her body. "I still can't believe you're actually going through with this."

Confused, Abby looked up. "What, scuba diving?" Sure, she was still too chicken to follow him in most of his athletic pursuits, but she'd taken the classes and been okay.

He tilted her chin. "No. Taking a risk on me."

"Sweetheart," she began, making the truest statement of her life. "Loving you is the surest thing I've ever done."

A word about the author…

Award winning author, Melissa Klein, writes heartwarming romance. She uses southern charm and humor to create everyday heroes who fight extraordinary battles. When away from the laptop, she gardens, creates pottery, and takes care of her loved ones. You can visit Melissa's website at

http://www.melissakleinromance.com

Thank you for purchasing
this publication of The Wild Rose Press, Inc.
For questions or more information
contact us at
info@thewildrosepress.com.
The Wild Rose Press, Inc.
www.thewildrosepress.com

www.ingramcontent.com/pod-product-compliance
Lightning Source LLC
Chambersburg PA
CBHW071006280626
47160CB00015B/1429